# Wine from the Emerald Tree

*Louise Shelley*

First published 2018
by Rowanvale Books Ltd
The Gate
Keppoch Street
Roath
Cardiff
CF24 3JW
www.rowanvalebooks.com

A CIP catalogue record for this book is available from the British Library.
ISBN: 978-1-911569-97-8

*There are some secrets which do not permit themselves to be told… mysteries which will not suffer themselves to be revealed.*

Edgar Allan Poe

# Author's Note

Although inspired by an actual event and based on historical fact, the names, characters and incidents portrayed in this work are the products of the author's imagination.

# Acknowledgements

My father for teaching me to have compassion and consideration for others and instilling me with a sense of ambition.

My husband, William, to whom I owe an incredible amount, for his love, understanding and support throughout many years of marriage.

My friend Mei Lin Ng for her excellent feedback and encouragement, without whom this book would never have been written.

My grandfather Frederick Diamond, who unfortunately I never knew, as his life was cut short due to his work in the mines, but I know would have been immensely proud of me.

To all miners who gave their lives to the mining industry, which powered the industrial revolution, and their families who suffered as a result.

Jane Lewis, whose life brutally ended in 1862.

# Chapter 1

Gaby threw her small holdall onto the narrow single bed before flinging herself next to it. She took some moments to appreciate her solace, valuing the sense of peace and inner calm. She was unused to this stillness of mind; relaxation eluded her more and more lately. Her mind was often distant and troubled by imaginings she was sure maturity would unveil as trivial. She always seemed to be surrounded by an atmosphere of impending events. Anxieties sometimes formed a stone that lay heavily in the pit of her stomach. Her thoughts were shadows thrown onto a wall, as if by the flickering light of a candle, where they danced teasingly, like butterflies fluttering out of reach of the ineffectual paw of a grabbing cat.

She was looking forward to some space away from the house she lived in with her parents and brother. She lay back on the bed, allowing her eyes to wander languidly around the room of her grandmother's house. A room as familiar to her as a cell to a long-serving prisoner. She knew every hairline crack. The stain on the wallpaper, like a map of Greenland, where she had once splashed blackcurrant cordial. The attempted crayon drawing of a tiger, a remnant of her childhood artistic endeavours, now hidden by a wardrobe. The small hole in the wall where a nail had once held something.

Her eyes rested on the ceiling. It was a blank

white canvas on which her mind had previously painted many images. There was nothing to paint at the moment, however. She noticed the lightshade's blue cornflowers and cotton frills, which she could touch if she stood on the bed. They'd feel like soft, silky cobwebs against the tips of her fingers. She turned her head to look at the picture of a pastoral scene that decorated one wall. It was said to have been painted by a former relative who had lived at the house when it was a farm cottage. Many generations of her family had farmed here. The farm was probably the reason her grandfather was still alive, unlike her paternal grandfather, whose lungs had been strangled by coal dust. She brought her thoughts back to the painting and wondered whether the fields it depicted belonged to Ty Coch. Whichever direction she looked in outside the cottage, however, she could find no resemblance to the painted lands.

She cast her eyes around the room once again. Letting the images evoked by these familiar objects flow over her, soothing her until all tension had left her body, she sank a little deeper into the mattress. Her light sleep was broken by her grandmother's voice, cutting the rope of her pleasant interlude so that it drifted away from her and was soon out of sight.

'Gabrielle!' her grandmother called, using the formal version of her name, as did many adults. 'Your Uncle Brian's home.'

Gaby leapt from the bed and rushed to the dressing table mirror, where she attempted to make herself look presentable. She was quickly running a comb through her hair when something suddenly caught her attention. The room in the reflection was not the one she was standing in. *But that's impossible*, she thought, as she turned to check behind her for reassurance. The room in the mirror was darker, gloomier, despite the walls being cream or possibly white. The plaster on the walls was irregular, and the rafters of the ceiling were exposed. The carpet was more like an oversized rug, which might have once been of rich, red hues but was now faded and worn, and covered large stone slabs. The furniture was of a heavy mahogany, and there was a large, metal-framed bed. Gaby could make out a heavy chest of drawers with brass handles. A bulky enamel bowl was on the surface of the drawers, resting on a circle of lace.

Gaby's eyes widened in amazement and her jaw went slack, for the person staring straight back into her eyes was not her.

It was a girl about her age, twenty, but her hair and clothes were unusual. Her hair was pinned loosely above her head. Her skirt was long and of thick, heavy cloth. Her blouse was white—not a bright white but slightly tinged with a brownish yellow, sepia almost, like the dry, crisp, old newspapers lining her grandmother's chest of drawers. The blouse was high at the neck with concertina pleats down the front and puffed sleeves.

The air Gaby breathed also felt different; it smelt stale and dusty. She scrutinised the room in the mirror, looking for something familiar. Where was the lightshade with cornflowers, and the blue curtains? The only item Gaby recognised was a brooch the girl wore, pinned high on the neck of the blouse. A circle of small rubies. Gaby had been given just such a brooch by her grandmother.

The girl in the mirror raised her hand and pointed her index finger directly at Gaby.

'Are you alright, dear?' the voice of Gaby's grandmother pierced her reverie, pulling her back to the present.

'Be there in a sec, Nan.'

Gaby turned back to the mirror but, despite checking carefully, all she could see reflected was herself and the room behind her. There were the blue cornflowers of the lightshade and the bed, which still bore her impression, all where they should be.

# Chapter 2

'Here's my girl! It's been over three weeks since your last visit.' Gaby's Uncle Brian grabbed her in a bear hug.

There was something reassuring about her Uncle Brian. He was of medium height and stocky, yet he seemed to somehow fill the room. His build meant he was well suited to rugby, a game he had played until he recently reached the age of forty. He was tough more than aggressive and his short black hair, which was slightly greying around the ears, was cut very close to his round, ruddy face and plump cheeks. Dark eyes peered through baby fat he appeared not to have shed. He always dressed very casually, but then, his lifestyle did not require any other form of dress. He worked as a plasterer for a small firm of local builders. His social life consisted of meeting his former rugby mates down the Seren, a pub at the bottom of the hill, four times a week and watching the local rugby match on Saturdays. His idea of dressing up was putting on a clean pair of jeans. He had lived with his parents at Ty Coch all of his life. There had been girlfriends, but they rarely lasted more than a few weeks, by which time they had all formed the opinion that he preferred the rugby lifestyle to them. Women had become the enemy of happiness as far as Brian was concerned.

Gaby, Brian and her grandfather Albert settled themselves around the lounge table whilst her grandmother busied herself in the kitchen. The lounge was elongated, as it consisted of two rooms merged into one. It still effectively consisted of a dining room and sitting area, the lounge chairs being situated in such a way as to form a barrier between the eating and television area. Photographs of Gaby and her brother, Jonathan, were displayed on top of the television, along with photographs of her mother and Brian on low side-cupboards and shelves. They were constant reminders of the past, exhibits of pride.

'Need any help, Nan?' Gaby called from the table.

'No, no, you just rest yourself, and let your Mamgu do all the work.'

Gaby's grandmother was a small yet sturdy woman. She wore her hair in a tight bun on top of her head, which maybe had something to do with the hard, determined look she had. She wore the tracks of her life on her face. She had seen much during her lifetime, but the wrinkled skin of her face and hands had a dignity, like that of the elderly working women in Russell Lee photographs. Her resilience was due to reserves built up to get through hard times. She was a survivor.

The blue veins of her grandmother's hands bulged as she laid the plates before them in an accomplished manner. She was used to under-taking more than one task at a time. She had looked after her parents and three children in Ty Coch, plunging clothes into the water of the enamel sink whilst keeping an eye on the children through the kitchen window as they ran amongst the chickens. Until they reached the age of six, that was, as then they helped out with chores on the farm.

Gaby's grandmother would huff indignantly on

hearing the term "working woman". 'Work!' she would exclaim, her voice a mixture of surprise and indignation. 'This generation don't know they're born, what with their microwaves and washing machines'.

Gaby's grandmother joined them at the table. Her grandfather and Brian had already helped themselves to bread and had tipped vegetables onto their plates. Gaby waited until they had finished their usual questioning regarding her mother, June, who was Brian's sister, her father, Clive, and brother, before deciding to broach the incident with the mirror, which had not left her mind throughout the teatime ritual.

'Nan?' Gaby tried to sound nonchalant. 'You know that lovely brooch you gave me?' There was a slight pause as she tried to gauge the mood. 'Where did you get it from?'

The atmosphere changed instantly. An uncomfortable silence fell across the table, a tension triggered by her careful question. Her grandfather and Brian exchanged a fleeting but loaded glance, before looking straight back down at their plates. There was no change to her grandmother's voice or movements, however.

'It was a family heirloom. It belonged to someone called Angharad. She used to work here.'

'Didn't she have children of her own?' Gaby asked cautiously.

'She died when she was twenty,' her grandmother replied flatly, without eye contact.

'My age!' said Gaby incredulously. 'How awful! How did she die?'

'Oh, it was a bad business.' There was a hint

of emotion in her grandmother's voice. 'She was murdered'.

'*What*?' Gaby was astounded. 'Who did it?'

'It was never found out.'

'Enough of this morbid talk,' her grandfather quickly intervened. 'Or you won't sleep tonight.'

He then proceeded to relate tales of the nightmares she'd had as a child. Her grandmother and Brian joined in with their own humorous anecdotes of such incidents. How she would flee screaming in her night dress, convinced there was someone in the room.

'"Oh, they're back again," we would all say,' her grandmother said laughingly.

Gaby realised there would be little benefit from pressing the issue further at this point, so she helped clear the table and wash the dishes whilst her grandmother talked of how her grandfather was keeping, and details of the neighbours' lives. Gaby's mind was elsewhere, however. Even though she heard her grandmother's voice, she did not register the words, which were just sounds; background noise, like the characterless music played in lifts and supermarket aisles.

After finishing the washing up, Gaby and her grandmother joined Brian and her grandfather, who were sitting comfortably around the television. Her grandmother took out her knitting needles, which she worked at with ease. Some current affairs programme was on the television, which Gaby was having difficulty focusing her attention on. The programme, however, triggered Brian and her grandfather into a political discussion.

'They can't do any worse in these parts than Thatcher did. Decimated the industry around here,' Gaby's grandfather declared with patriarchal authority.

'Not just around here,' Brian countered. 'Other parts of the country were also affected.'

The conversation took its usual course, with her grandfather referring to the miner's strike of 1926.

'We got them back in 1972 though, Dad.'

'Only to be thrashed again in 1984. That was the end of it; we never recovered,' her grandfather said with a melancholic air of resignation.

Gaby was not in the mood for such conversation; she therefore excused herself by saying she needed to unpack. Apprehension returned as soon as she entered the bedroom. She tried to distract her mind with the activity of unpacking. She only had a small amount of clothing, however—not much was required for a weekend stay.

She was the only one in the room, but she did not feel alone. Quite a few times in her life, she had felt she had company despite there being no visible sign. It was not a comforting presence, not like the security she felt when Brian was around. Neither, however, did she feel any threat. This feeling had come to her more and more often lately.

'You're on your own too much,' her grandmother used to chide. 'You should be out with girls your own age, having fun.' She'd never mixed well with others, however. She had a few close friends, of whom others would enquire how they got on so well. 'She's odd,' some would say. 'That doesn't mean she's a bad person,' her friends would defensively reply. 'She's different, but so what?'

She checked the mirror again before turning off the light. There was no sign of anything other than herself and the room behind her. *Oh well,* she shrugged. *Maybe it was my overactive imagination.*

She got into bed but was in that uncomfortable state where sleep was unobtainable. Her mind still reflected the image of the girl in the mirror, an image that had never really left her mind throughout the evening. The sounds emanating from the television turned into a drone, and sleep finally overpowered her.

# Chapter 3

Gaby awoke the next morning, refreshed and invigorated. After anticipating a night of tossing and turning, she had slept remarkably well. She lay there for a while, straining to hear the sounds of the world outside, the faint honking of horns.

She was hit by the smell of bacon. The smell of cooking was ever-present in Ty Coch. *Nan must be preparing Brian's bacon butty*, thought Gaby, before making her way to the vertical line of light seeping through the narrow divide of the curtains.

She pulled apart the thick blue velvet to reveal a bright new day. Raw morning sunshine filled the room, like cold milk splashing onto a bowl full of cereal. She opened the window to let in the morning freshness of the mountainside. The day opened before her. Pure air tumbled into the room, transferring it from a place of sleep to an active reception room. The air smelt cleaner up here, and she let it wash over her.

Her grandmother was attending to her daily domestic routine when Gaby emerged from the bathroom, dressed in a pale green sweater and machine-faded jeans. Her thick, honey-blond hair rested on her shoulders. She had been blessed with smooth, unblemished skin.

The kitchen, which sloped gently upwards, was gilded by a yellow light. A builder colleague of Brian's had done a great deal of work on the kitchen two years ago. The cabinets were either low to the ground or higher on the wall, which gave the impression of spaciousness.

After gently embracing her grandmother, Gaby reached up and took a box of muesli from the cabinet.

'Oh, not that rabbit food,' her grandmother said admonishingly. 'Let me make you some bacon and eggs'.

'What are you trying to do, Nan? Clog up my arteries?'

'Go on with you, never harmed my generation. I've more energy than half this lot today. They spend half their time in front of the TV. You're far too thin as it is.'

Gaby sunk into an easy chair, where she continued to eat her muesli. She was not underweight for her five feet and four inches, though her slim figure may have been more a result of nervous energy than her healthy eating and exercise. She had a steady job, working in the accounts department of a nearby town. People around the area called it a town, but it would have been more like a village to a city dweller.

Now that she was alone with her grandmother, Gaby took the opportunity to find out a little more about Angharad. She was intrigued by the strong impression the subject seemed to have aroused at the dinner table the previous evening. She cautiously considered how to phrase her next words.

'What did Angharad look like, Nan?' she said slowly,

'Don't know; she died before I was born,' her grandmother said in an even-toned voice.

'Is there a photograph anywhere?'

'Don't suppose they had cameras in those days. Anyway, what have you got planned for today?'

'I'm going to go to the library and, as it's nice at the moment, I thought I'd walk up to the top to get the bus.'

'You make sure you wrap up well then. There's still a chill in the air even though the sun is out, and you know how quickly the weather can change.'

'Yeah, OK, and what are you going to do this morning?'

'Need you ask? The washing, the cleaning and the cooking. Tadcu will be down the allotment all morning. Brian will be down the bookies.'

'I never understand why Dado needs an allotment; there's so much land here.'

'It's somewhere to chat, init. The men do a bit of digging then lean on their spades to talk about the comings and goings of the village, putting the world to rights. Besides, I wouldn't want a vegetable patch in the garden—looks scruffy. He brought some nice beans back the other week, though. Swapped them with Bernie for potatoes.'

'Quite a market economy they have going there.'

Gaby's grandfather Albert was over six foot, with a weather-beaten face. His hair was grey and still thick, despite his advanced age. He never stooped when he walked but was always tall and erect. He had a moustache, smoked a pipe and, despite having put on weight over the years, was still relatively slim. He wore a flat, cloth cap, as did the other men who spent time at the allotment exchanging wisdom. These caps rarely left their heads outside the home.

The kitchen had already started to resemble a chemical laboratory by the time Gaby was ready to leave. Pots and pans filled with bubbling liquids. Vapours were being released that would permeate the rooms with a comforting aroma.

'Are you coming back for lunch?' She heard her grandmother say, through teeth clamped on a peg, whilst hanging out the washing on the garden line.

'I'll get a sandwich or something from the Centre,' Gaby replied and, from the corner of her eye, caught her grandmother shaking her head.

# Chapter 4

Gaby liked the early part of the mornings when no one else was around. She relished her own space. Alone, she could be queen of her own empire, free to create whatever world she wanted. She received the fresh breath of the breeze. Her grandparents' cottage was on the side of the mountain, which was referred to as a hill, in a part of the village known as Brynhalig. Some of the older inhabitants referred to the hill as Brynpyrs. There were other houses in the distance, which she would see in about ten minutes.

The hill that separated the two villages seemed to have erupted and pushed through the earth's surface like a determined volcano. Gaby had almost reached the top when she stopped to survey the village to which she belonged. She was unable to articulate the affinity she felt with the land. She did not understand it herself, familiarity on an unfamiliar level. She had a kind of love-hate relationship with her home town. The beauty surrounding her, though, could also be a source of frustration.

Both villages could be seen from here. She rarely visited the other village, like most of each village's inhabitants. They felt there was no need to.

The valley looked as if it had been sculpted by a huge caterpillar of ice. A caterpillar that had forced its way towards a destination, churning up rocks and boulders on its route, designing the landscape. A caterpillar that had created geological structures, forming channels for rivers to flow through. The Ice Age had left its mark on the village as good as any calling card—steep, glacial escarpments, further carved by rain and river erosion. The river wound its way around the bottom of the village like a supple string, a trough for the verdant blaze, which was to become the village.

The walk over the fields gave Gaby's mind a chance to recuperate. Her thoughts could be so intense that it sometimes seemed they would overload her head, and she would not be able to cope with the weight of even a wafer-thin sliver of a thought. Here, however, she felt at one with nature, and was able to lose herself to the present. In the summer months, she would walk barefoot along the grass. Feeling the texture under her soles, this gave the sensation of walking across a vast, open plain.

Many would find this walk through upwardly sloping fields a strenuous task, but Gaby ambled easily over the plants, grasses and small rocks. These products of the mountains had provided her childhood entertainment. The ferns and tall grasses had supplied great hiding places. Many a time, juvenile exploits had scraped the skin from her knees. The dry-stone wall boundaries had become castle ramparts.

Ferns and gorse competed here for attention, greenery made opulent by abundant rainfall. The green shoots held the promise of an impending summer. The summer sun, however, would dehydrate the grass and heather to dry skin, rendering the foliage an arsonist's toy. Some teenagers in these parts found great amusement in setting the mountainside alight, thus depriving the slopes of months of greenery.

Gaby stopped for a while to breathe in the aroma of soaked leaves and menthol. The delicious freshness of a late-spring morning. She would savour such moments in the years to come, when reminiscence would become her favoured form of entertainment. She could almost taste the season on her tongue. The menthol came from the serried ranks of carefully cultivated conifers, standing to attention over many sides of the village. Strategically placed to cover up the scars of industrialisation, cosmetic surgery on a once-thriving industrial workstation. An artificial landscape, based on a human concept, intended to create a place of natural beauty, and to purify the atmosphere after industrialism had blackened the air and transformed the rivers to moving tar. The conifers were now as native to the village as the bluebells and wandering, white sheep. Sheep were hardy animals and the only inhabitants on some slopes, where it was felt nothing could be built. Gaby had spent many an hour alone here, feeling safe as long as she was in sight of the houses.

She was now at the highest point of Brynhalig, where she could survey the expanse of the village below. Even at about three miles distance, the church spire was instantly recognisable, pointing skyward in the way a compass needle always points north. The spire was the tallest building in the village, as it had been from the time it was built in the eighteen hundreds. A dour, imposing building, built not to be ignored. A fine example of spiritual engineering. A constant reminder, overlooking the village, that there was no escaping the watchful presence.

The road meandered in a long, winding descent down to the bottom of the hill, where it joined the one main road, which ran like an artery through the whole group of linear villages. Other roads branched off, like veins flowing through the many side streets, densely populated by houses that had sprung up to provide shelter for the influx of workers required by the burgeoning coal industry over a century ago.

A housing estate had been spread over the summit of Brynhalig, like icing over the top of a cake. Blobs of brutal concrete dotted densely together. The type of housing that had been inspired by utopian schemes of modernist architects and planners of the sixties. A Corbusian vision of neat, cubist blocks. Councils had been encouraged to fill landscapes with these purpose-built houses. Mass produced, standardised, as if straight from a production line. Building firms had received subsidies to build quickly, and had done so carelessly, with a lack of foresight, the emphasis being on the short-term. Panels were produced that slotted together like jigsaw pieces, enabling homogenised buildings to be repeated and replicated throughout the country, monochrome and featureless.

Once hailed as icons of modernity, these harsh housing estates had been left to decay. A monolith of concrete, stark outlines against the sky, ignorant of their environmental surroundings.

Brynhalig was a conflict between nature and domesticity. How could this unrestrained landscape be tamed? Not since the Stone Age had any construction succeeded on this terrain. Mine owners had tried, but even with the boundless motivation of greed, they could not impose their industrial edifices on this land that was hostile to human interference.

Concrete was believed to have strength and security, but it had not aged gracefully. Elements thrashed and crashed against civilisation. The buildings and their habitants remained, however, wilted and tarnished, overlooking the village, defying and challenging.

Gaby entered the estate, which many in the villages below would see as entering a foreign country.

'*What do you want to go into that place for?*' her father would rebuke. '*All drugs and crime.*'

'*It's not that bad, Dad,*' she would counter. '*Kelly lives there, and all her family are decent working people.*'

Kelly was a childhood friend of Gaby's; they were happy to see each other on the coincidental occasions they passed in the village, despite having drifted apart in their early teens. They spoke of each other with fondness, regardless of their differences. They accepted each other.

'*It won an award when first completed,*' her mother remarked. She had worked for the housing department of the local council, before she resigned to run a pub with Clive.

'*Whoever gave the award needs their head read,*' Clive replied.

'*I suppose it looked good on an architect's sketch pad,*' June replied. '*The ideals were fine, to provide housing for the poor. But stuck up there, isolated and abandoned, is it any wonder that crime flourished? They probably felt immune from the law.'*

*'Oh come on,'* Gaby said imploringly. *'They're not all bandits living there. Some of them are really nice.'*

*'The place should have been knocked down years ago,'* Gaby's father muttered reprovingly before turning back to his newspaper.

Gaby had spent much of her childhood in this area, however, and had once played with the children on the mountainside. She noticed some children playing now, cheerfully huddled together, oblivious of the hard lives that lay ahead.

The community square was always busy on a Saturday morning, whilst people went about their weekend rituals. This was the interchange for passengers changing buses to go from one village to the other, if they needed to for work or to visit relatives.

The single mums were out in force today. Pushing prams as their forebears once pushed trolleys full of coal. Gaby wondered how they could stand their lives of daily drudgery. The feeding and dressing of children. The endless amount of washing and struggle on a limited budget, surrounded by dreary council concrete. Women in their thirties walked past. The luminosity had left their skin. *They're probably grandmothers*, Gaby thought as she wandered a little way further into the main square. A small area the planners referred to as the Precinct.

The space contained some featureless, unwelcoming shops, which would be behind armoured shutters after seven P.M. Discarded crisp and cigarette packets drifted across the grey paving, whilst men, young and old, entered and emerged from betting shops, clutching slips of paper between nicotine-stained fingers.

Gaby went into the amenity store to pick up some sandwiches and crisps to eat whilst waiting for the bus.

'Hello, Mrs Hopkins,' she greeted the middle aged woman in overalls behind the counter.

'Oh hello, Gabrielle—haven't seen you for a while. How's that grandmother of yours?'

'Oh bearing up.'

'She's a battler that one.'

'How are you keeping?'

'So-so, can't complain. I have the shop and Harry, even though he can be a nuisance at times.'

'How are the boys?'

'Kevin—well, not much shape there. Supposed to be helping me in the shop. Where is he now? In bed no doubt. Probably stroll in lunchtime gone. Mark, he's in the army. Hated it at first, but getting used to it. Money in his pocket, see, drinking with the army lads on weekends. Better than being in this place, he says.'

'Well at least he's got a job. Nice to have seen you—bye!'

'And to have seen you too, luv. Give my love to your grandmother. Bye!'

A straggle of young boys loitered aimlessly outside the off-licence. Gaby's attention was caught by some bold, colourful graffiti on one of the walls. Attempts by frustrated youths to stamp their individuality on a blank canvas, like the primitive art once found on the inside of caves. These youths were waiting for something to happen in their lives, however inconsequential. They were young teens, never long without a cigarette between their fingers. The cigarette had become an accessory almost, a sign of teenage sophistication.

This was an estate where teenagers had a shelf life. Programmed to self-destruct, death by drugs or alcohol.

Two girls walked past with round, extended abdomens, ready to give birth to tomorrow's deprived generation. They couldn't have been older than seventeen. This uniform, contained world of teenagers' young, but old.

Gaby wondered whether they had imagined that their lives would end up being this way, as their minds wandered from the chalk letters on the blackboard. Gaby had daydreamed of being a teacher. Maybe these youths had no choice. This was all they could hope for, and the only life they saw. Assumptions were made, and no one told them about university, as they were not expected to get that far. The pit or the factory was their only option, and even those opportunities were gradually diminishing. They were unaware of a life beyond the walls of the estate.

They became conditioned to accept the estate as their destiny. Moulded and shaped by the fading colours, the substance of their surroundings became them. Afflicted by a social malaise and estranged from employment by lack of skills. They passed this hopelessness and apathy to their children, whilst still children themselves. A perpetual circle, subjected to powerless policies.

*We need not be the products of our past*, thought Gaby. How could such knowledge be imparted to these unfortunate souls, however, trapped by insularity and circumstance?

# Chapter 5

Gaby boarded the bus for the library. From the top of the bus, where she was level with the second floor windows of the two-tier houses, she saw a different world. She could see over garden walls and glimpse the inhabitants' lives in their contents. Some contained innovative creations in bricolage, which were built to house pigeons or chickens. Others belonged to keen gardeners and looked like artists' palettes, with blobs of colour from variegated species of plants and flowers.

She disembarked in what locals thought of as the commercial centre of the village. This was where most of the enterprise seemed to coagulate—the shops, cafes and youth centre. Although there were pubs all over the villages, this was the meeting place of the young. Here was where they struggled to create a vibrancy for the weekend.

The library was a modern building, built in the sixties, in stark contrast to the colliery hall that stood opposite. The colliery hall was a grandiose structure, with cultural references to ancient architecture, such as Doric columns and arched doorways. Its original purpose was to entertain the thousands of immigrants who flooded the area in search of work, following the discovery of coal.

When the mines closed, so did many shops. Businesses left the villages, never to return.

While some coal communities had developed a mutual life support system—introducing new enterprises to replace coal, attempting to prevent chaos with commerce—this village's life blood had dried. The community and businesses that had once filled the whole village were now concentrated in this one area. Inside, the library was light, airy, modern, and seemed immense, despite the numerous lengths of bookshelves. The main library consisted of two open floors, the upper floor being smaller than the lower, more like a shelf itself. Both floors shared the roof and the skylight, from which sunlight flooded from on high. The reference library was a separate section and, although small in comparison to the main library, was still a relatively large area. Silence and solemnity hung in the air like a heavy drape, however, making the room seem smaller than it actually was.

A small, slim woman with short dark hair and an enthusiastic expression moved swiftly towards Gaby.

'Can I help you?' she asked keenly.

'You might. I'm looking for information on a murder that took place in Brynhalig, of someone called Angharad.'

'The Ty Coch murder.' The librarian's eyes sparked to life as if lit by the flick of a switch.

Gaby's heart quickened, and she nodded, eagerly awaiting the next sentence.

'Oh yes, caused quite a stir around these parts. Nothing much happens around here now, but it was even less in those days. The mines were only just starting up. Before the mines, it was just farmers and sheep. Best place to begin would be the newspapers. They are all held on microfiche.' The librarian hastened over to a wall of small, wooden drawers. 'They are all in chronological order. Here we are.' Her voice slowed down as she scrutinised the labels on the drawers. '1850… 1859… 1862… Should be in here.' She triumphantly pulled open the drawer. 'It was about early summer time, if I remember rightly,' she said whilst shuffling through the contents of the drawer. 'So around here.'

'Thanks.' Gaby smiled fleetingly, moving her fingers to the place indicated, impatient for the librarian to return to her desk.

She put the first slide of May under the machine. Much of the news seemed to be centred around the extension of the railway line and the intended expansion of the coal industry in the area. Her eyes followed the sentences on the screen. There was much buoyant speculation on how this would change the way of life in the villages. This topic continued over the following slides. The chapels seemed to have played a large part in the community. Sunday schools provided education to children as well as being places of worship. The humdrum nature of the task had a mesmerising effect on Gaby, until she reached a headline that leapt from the June slide.

*MURDER MOST FOUL*

The heading had the starkness of an abstract painting. Gaby, who was resting her weight onto her left elbow, lunged towards the microfiche screen, as if thrown by the force of a catapulted stone.

*The body of Angharad Morgan was found in the early hours of the morning. Drenched in blood,*

31

*her throat had been cut to the extent that it was practically severed from her body.*

The rest of the article disclosed that Angharad had failed to return to the farm where she worked and lived with her uncle and aunt, after leaving to meet her fiancé, Owen Thomas, on the way to church. Owen Thomas turned up at the farm around eight P.M, as she had not been at their appointed meeting place or at church. He was in an agitated state and went to look for her. Her aunt became suspicious around eleven o'clock when neither Angharad nor Owen had returned to the farm. She alerted her husband, Llewellyn Morgan, and Gwyn Evans, a young farmhand who also lived at the farm, and they both set out to look for Angharad. To their horror, they came across Angharad's body, which lay lifeless on a track not far from the farm. Their lamplight revealed a large area of the ground around her body was stained by blood. Llewellyn gently shook the body, at which point the head practically fell away from the shoulders. Llewellyn took Gwyn to a friend's house before running down to the village to summon help.

Llewellyn Morgan hurried back to the scene with a Police Constable who found, on further examination, that Angharad's throat had been cut from ear to ear. A razor lay about three feet from the body.

Gaby desperately wanted to find out more, but on checking her watch, she was shocked to realise she had stayed fifty minutes longer than she had intended. She had arranged to meet her boyfriend, Mickey, thirty minutes ago.

# Chapter 6

Mickey was waiting outside their usual Saturday afternoon meeting place, leaning against the wall of the cafe.

'Got lost did you?' he said casually.

'You'll never believe what I've just found out.'

'It had better be good. A benefactor has left you a fortune?'

They took a seat by one of the Formica-topped tables. The place exuded sixties kitsch. A cafe that had not changed its clothes since that time. Neither of them had yet reached the age for such reminiscence.

Gaby had been seeing Mickey for over a year now. He worked in a factory, but he would have liked to have been a mechanic, as he loved cars. He also loved music, and he had recently bought a guitar, which he practised playing with his friend Bobbit every Tuesday evening. Despite being two years her junior, he was a deep thinker. She had felt his sensitivity soon into their courtship. Such a person was difficult to find in these parts. Unlike many other people, he did not see her as strange.

Though she looked forward to their time together, spent discussing films, books, and music, he seemed far more committed to the relationship. She had plans beyond a future together. She had no intention of falling into the cycle of work, marriage, children then death.

Gaby liked Mickey because he was different.

He was uncontaminated by ambition, so she appreciated his admiration of this quality in her. Maybe, he represented what was lacking in her life. Other people tasted the past differently to her but, in Mickey, she felt she had found someone who could share her world. At last she had found someone whose idea of life was not to get drunk every weekend, and whose aim was not to try to get every girl into bed as quickly as possible.

Mickey, at six foot two, was taller than the average village male. Being quite slim, his height gave him a loose, gangly appearance. He also wore black quite a lot, which did not help to make him look as if he had a larger build. The colour appealed to him—though, as he was fond of saying, "Black is not a colour." He also dyed his hair black, which gave it a glossy shine. His skin was somewhat pale, so he came across as quite striking. He was attractive in an unconventional way, with eyes of liquid tar, full of expression, which were framed by long, luxurious eyelashes. His teeth were slightly uneven, which added interest to his angular features, unlike the bland, perfect smiles of the boy bands that had smiled down from the posters that had adorned her bedroom wall in her schooldays.

Gaby zealously proceeded to recount the recent occurrences, from the appearance of the girl in the mirror to the newspaper article in the library. Words spilled rapidly from her mouth.

Mickey's eyes widened with mock surprise. 'So you're sharing a room with a ghost now!' he said with a bemused look.

'What do you think she was trying to tell me'?

'Maybe she was saying it's her room tonight.'

'Oh, you're not taking this seriously.'

'I think you've had enough excitement for today. Finish your coffee, and let's get some fresh mountain air. Clear your head a bit.'

They left the cafe in a bright mood—Mickey playful, and Gaby invigorated with excitement. They turned down the high street, walking jauntily whilst taking the time to enjoy each other's company. Mickey, sometimes striding ahead, would turn and face Gaby and amuse her with witty quips, to which she tried to retaliate.

They soon left the streets behind, and walked on a flattened, discarded wasteland that had once been an industrial estate. Factories had been placed here as a result of government inducements, attempts to fill the gaping holes left by the mines. Now the site was derelict, the sharp steel of progress left rotting. A pile of rusting rubble, of crumbled, fallen factories. Tufts of grass grew between great, broken slabs of concrete. A site meant for better things, the purpose of which had long been forgotten.

This place, which had once teemed with noise and activity, now had the hushed vacancy of desertion. A lost, ruined city.

There were many such landscapes throughout the villages. Places where vegetation could not grow, not even weeds. Useless slagheaps, detritus from the mines. The arrival of coal had once turned this area into an industrial workshop, attracted by an inexhaustible supply of trees. Skylines had been changed overnight by winding towers, the skeletons of which still remained. Mountainsides became instant ghettos of grimy houses. Roads ripped through tiny villages. Farmers sold land to investors, who profited from speculators, turning good-quality grazing land into industrial sprawl. The coal industry's decline had been almost as rapid as its growth.

Gaby and Mickey had been walking for about fifteen minutes when the land returned to green. The conifers had performed their job well, and grown to great heights. Although the land was green, it was too regimented, too artificial. A green coating spread over the land, in the same way Brian made walls more presentable with a coating of plaster.

The incline of the mountain began, gentle at first, but soon became steeper. Gaby looked up to where the mists merged the mountain with the sky. The clouds above them were sponges of wetness waiting to be squeezed, and were uniting into a menacing grey. She speculated how long it would be before the rain fell—a calculation she was accomplished at making—and predicted they had about an hour.

They passed the last house before the curving swell of the mountain. It was a grand house, which had once belonged to a mine owner. Nestled here amongst the trees, away from the stains of neglect. It would have once been boastful and ornate, built to be noticed. A landmark to the prosperity that rewards enterprise—not like the tightly packed, square, miner's cottages, all built with the same un-complex thought.

There were many such houses dotted over the villages. They stood out starkly, like exotic plants, as once the rising, steel structures of the mines must have contrasted sharply with the abundant greenery of the undulating hills. Porticos of grooved pillars, windows protruding outwards like swollen growths

*What would have taken place in a house such as this?* Gaby wondered. Elaborate dinners, tables abundantly laid, dressed in finery, glinting sherry glasses being raised before roaring fireplaces of pink marble. Unrestrained extravagance, whilst those around them lived in poverty and squalor.

Mickey's grandmother had once worked in such an establishment. She had been one of the maidservants, summoned by the bells to perform ostentatious rituals, serving meals of epicurean proportions on shiny silver trays. She'd regaled Gaby with tales of lavish feasts, foods she had never seen before, where she had first tasted grapes. Mickey and his sister had heard these stories many times, but Gaby was enthralled. She encouraged their grandmother to speak of these times. She would talk of conversations overheard at the dinner table. How they tried to justify the conditions of their workers:

*'Nonsense. Pay them more! They will only squander it on alcohol. Keep their wages low and they will work harder. That bumbling fool Asquith should have stood his ground.'*

The ground beneath Gaby's feet turned from tarmac to asphalt. They had reached the forestry road, conveniently cut into the side of the mountain by the Forestry Commission to enable access to areas otherwise inaccessible by maintenance vehicles. The road was crumbling now, a victim of erosion. Gaby and Mickey could see nothing either side of them, apart from the light breaking through the dense conifers. Tall, identical timbers, keeping out the rest of the world, forming a curving corridor around the track, which made Gaby think of a maze of hedgerows she had once seen as a child in the garden of a former mine owner's house. Those not brought up amongst these mountains could easily get lost.

The trees were so closely packed together that they were impossible to walk through. Only dogs could reach the interior, where nothing but mushrooms grew. Gaby's dog had used to run, crashing through the foliage, and she'd wished she could follow, although the darkness sent a chill of fear through her. The only light was sun points penetrating the pine needles, specks of gold strewn like coins across the forest floor. Two months hence, they would throw their summer shadows like spears across the loose gravel of the track.

The trees cleared and the roughshod road came to an abrupt end where rubble met grass. This point would have caused confusion to anyone unfamiliar with the area, who would turn back, unaware that there was much more on display. The only sounds here were those of nature, the monotone buzzing of grasshoppers. The stillness forced one to contemplate the surroundings. A three-dimensional view of the village lay out below. Dwellings, distinct at first, blurred into trees and green in the distance, forming a surrealist painting, framed by the sweeping, arcing swell of the mountains.

Gaby and Mickey clambered up the grassy, almost perpendicular, slope with the grace of two mountain goats impervious to a dazzling sun. They sank to the ground on reaching the end of their climb, shoulders lifting and ribcages swelling and subsiding with the effort of sucking in air to satiate their thirsty lungs. The air tasted different here, as pure and refreshing as a cold drink on a hot day.

They contemplated the village below whilst their breathing slowed to a comfortable pace. Microscopic people and cars below them, milling about like dots on a screen from a computer game. From this point, the mountains had lost their might. The white house of the former mine owner now looked like a rabbit, nestled amongst long grass.

'Doesn't look much up here does it?' said Mickey

'Looks like a play set. I saw a film once where the gods in the clouds could just reach down, pick up ships and move them to somewhere else.'

'Wish I could do that with the school near me,' said Mickey sardonically. 'Kids are running amok in the close.'

'I expect they'll be closing it soon. I hear they're closing my old junior's. It's half empty now. There were kids practically hanging out the windows when I was there.'

'Speaking of kids, Bobbit's girlfriend's pregnant.'

'He's bought into that cliché has he? Sixteen years of toil and struggle at least. He can forget all his plans about forming a band. His time will be taken up with trying to reason with Kate over what shoes to buy for the baby. "The designer ones look so cute,"' she said in a mocking imitation of Kate. She switched to a deeper tone of voice, '"But they cost half my wage love, and he'll grow out of them in two weeks." *Ooh*, she'll say.' She clasped her hands to her chest as her voice shot up an octave. '"But his feet sticking out of the pram will look so pretty."'

'Don't suppose he'll be joining us down at the Emerald on a Friday any more. Just as well, he'll probably be talking about how many centimetres the baby has grown.'

'I expect he'll be talking about divorce in ten years' time.'

'As much as ten,' Mickey said with mock surprise. 'You don't have much faith in marriage do you?'

'Depressing, isn't it.'

'Almost as depressing as the view from here. What are we? A road to nowhere, with houses either side.'

They fell silent, just the sound of the breeze through the trees and telegraph wires behind them. A soft strum played the wires like a harp, accompanied by the gentle, tambourine rustle of the conifers, and the faint sound of horns from far down below, with short spaces in between.

'I used to spend a lot of time up here,' said Mickey, lost in thought, 'Away from the unkindness of the human race. Watching the cars and people going by, wondering where they were going.'

'No mystery there,' said Gaby sarcastically. 'Going to the shop for a tin of something, pack of chewing gum or cigarettes, to the pub or rushing home to watch the match or latest soap episode.'

'Imagine a world without cars,' Mickey said dreamily.

'There'd be less pollution for one thing, and people would probably be less fat.'

'Did you know cars are formed from materials produced by the universe? So if the universe is thirteen point eight billion years old, then so must cars be.'

'No wonder your Dad's car is falling apart then.'

'Where do you hope to be in ten years' time?' said Mickey.

'Not here, that's for sure.'

'Would you marry for money?'

'No, definitely not. I'm not that desperate to get out. Anyway, we'd better get moving; we don't want to be stuck here when the rains come.'

A pileup of thick grey cloud had turned the village sullen, but they got up in a lighter mood; it was a relief to be walking on flat ground. The undulations of a tumulus became noticeable underfoot. Emotions stirred in Gaby, as they always did in certain places such as this.

'I don't think anyone can walk past this point without stopping,' said Gaby distantly. 'No matter how many times one has seen it.'

'A stone age camp, thrown up by ancient people,' said Mickey drily.

'Apparently, it's a rare example of an iron age hill fort.'

'Just looks like a pile of stones to me. Collapsed houses. I've seen rubble like this in many a backyard.'

'What is beneath us is history,' said Gaby wistfully. 'People eking out an existence, carving tools with stones.'

'The only people to have lived on top of a mountain since have been the people of Brynhalig, and they haven't evolved much either.'

'Life is a matter of chance. People can't help their circumstances I suppose.'

The sky had turned into a grey slab. Change

was perpetually above them. Dull, compacted clouds prompted them to begin their descent to the other side of the mountain. Walking downwards required a different set of skills. They needed to concentrate on their footholds, tentatively feeling for the ground beneath them. Encased toes trying to grip the ground, as Bushmen gripped the trunks of trees to reach the fruit. Flicks of icy rain pricked at their cheeks, like aqueous thorns.

'Here it comes,' said Mickey

'The last place we want to be caught in a storm is here,' said Gaby, as the spots of rain against their skin became more frequent. 'Come on; let's get to the shepherd house.'

Grappling with grass and plants below them, they scrambled down the hill, which was slowly turning into a ski slope. They managed to get onto a mountain path, only to find it had been turned glutinous by water. The rain became relentless and persistent, and they battled with the resisting wind to reach their safe haven, which poked through the ground like a molehill.

'Thank goodness for sheep,' exclaimed Mickey on reaching the wooden door of the cubed stone hut, which was saturated with moisture.

Gaby stopped before following Mickey inside and looked up at the attacking rain, hurling itself straight at the ground. The wind repelled like an opposing magnet, sending sheets of rain off course, like a curtain being parted.

'Get in here, you idiot.' Mickey dragged her into the hut, 'Trying to get yourself pneumonia. I'm not that bad, surely?'

Gaby peeled off her thin rain-jacket, which clung to her like cellophane. She hung it on a spike on the wall and sat on the makeshift stone bench. Light struggled through a narrow slit of unglazed window in the thick stone wall. The one-roomed hut smelt of damp and dead leaves. A resting place for sheep, not humans. She licked the water from her lips and thought, *So this is what freshness tastes like*. Sometimes she wondered if she was too used to chemicals and synthetics.

Mickey sat alongside her and placed his arm around her shoulders. He quietly took in the atmosphere of seclusion, breathing in the subtle tang of her perfume, aware of the points of contact where their bodies met. He felt her warmth seep through her two layers of clothing. Many people thought her aloof and pretentious. His sister found her strange. *"She's a snob,"* his friend Bobbit would say, *"thinks she's something special. Life owes her something."* Yet Mickey found her unique. He liked the fact that she was ambitious. Someone with a bit of go, was how he phrased it. Not one of these women whose aim in life was to get married and have children. Treating men like lumps of meat was how he saw such women. He felt her body against his become heavier with relaxation. He felt privileged at being allowed into her world. They sat protected from the fury of the rain being hurled at the hut, watching some of it crawl down the walls.

'Anything happening in work at the moment?' Mickey broke the silence.

'The same ledgers to be updated. I expect I'll go in Monday and have to listen to Alicia's exploits of her weekend. Mandy will spend the first half hour discussing the cat and Coronation Street. How about you?'

'I try not to think about it too much. Pulling the press handle, day in, day out. If I thought about it, I would go mad. I'd be in an asylum by now if it wasn't for the radio.'

The slowing drumbeat of the rain had come to a complete stop.

'We'd better go now,' Gaby said, 'whilst we have the chance.'

The light outside was grey, but the surroundings always felt different after the rain, fresh and renewed, a house after a good spring-clean. Rain dissolves, nourishes and heals. The dark clouds had melted into a mist that hung on the mountains.

'So that's one part of the cycle.' Gaby scanned the sky and mountains. 'Rain flows down the mountains, to the river, to the sea. The sun evaporates the rain back up to the clouds, ready for the next bout of rain. Nature's industry— nothing is superfluous in nature. Only, nature hasn't messed up like man's industry,' she said, somewhat reproachfully.

'Don't try to find the point to it all,' said Mickey.

They strolled through the dripping trees until they reached the bus stop at the village, where they kissed before parting.

The afternoon light was just beginning to darken when Gaby arrived at Ty Coch with a feeling of satisfaction. She was looking forward to giving thought to what she had found out at the library. As she distinctly heard the sound of three notes of playful laughter, she stopped suddenly. She swivelled around sharply, just in time to see a young woman wearing thick, heavy clothes disappear around the side of the cottage.

Gaby raced after her, but when she turned the

corner, there was no other person in sight. She rushed around the rest of the cottage, even though logic told her there was no way someone could get around the other side in such a short time. On finding no one, she surveyed the unoccupied fields. Her eyes strained for a glimpse of the figure, which seemed to have disappeared into the ether. There was a strange eeriness to the stillness and emptiness, as she tried to make sense of it all.

# Chapter 7

Two figures scrambled excitedly up the mountainside, faces glowing with delight and the bracing air. The woman, slightly ahead of the man, hair flying, hitched up her heavy cloth skirt and many layered petticoats. Nimbly negotiating the huge tree roots splayed beneath her, instinct enabled her to travel at such speed. A person less familiar with the terrain would have needed to apply far more care and attention.

The man following wore a jacket of thick cloth and a flat cap. He took large strides to keep up with the woman. Every so often, she would turn back laughingly to look at him until eventually they were side by side, where they slowed their pace to a walk, their breath exhaling in gasps.

'I can give you a run for your money, Gwyn Evans.'

'Aye, you can do that, Bach, but I can shear a sheep better than you.'

'I can milk a cow better than you, and I bet with practice I could beat you at sheep shearing,' she said with fake indignation.

The mountain, which reached towards the clouds, was alive with the sound of birds, insects, and the cooing of courting wood pigeons. Spring's promise was a gentle, light gold caress. Shoots had punctured their way through the soil, happy to be out after a long winter's slumber. Buttercups, daisies, dandelions and delicate daffodils clung to the mountainside, forming a fecund coverlet. Bees hovered over clover; nature flourished here, everything bred. The sun busily radiated its energy, supplying nature with its requirements. Parts of the mountain were luxuriously wooded. Trees not planted by the hand of man, forests of such density as to render the woods sunless. The mountain looked proud then.

Angharad and Gwyn reached a clearing, which beckoned them with lush greenness. There was still a profusion of growth around them—waist-high ferns, clandestine places where they could be unobserved. Places that only attracted birds and other wildlife. Up here, they could easily become Adam and Eve.

Angharad took this as a time of respite, out of reach of the conflict that set her opposing thoughts in motion.

She had a fiancé, Owen, a serious young man with a good job in insurance. He had glistening, dark hair, meticulously combed close to his head and kept in place by oil. He dressed in dark suits tailored to his slim body, and white shirts with the small collar always buttoned down. A silk neckerchief tucked into his waistcoat. Shoes polished to a porcelain shine. Dark eyes that reminded her of the glass buttons she sometimes sewed onto her uncle's shirts.

Owen talked about the insurance trade with optimism. Coal had just been discovered in the area. *'Things are going to change around here,'* he would muse. And things were changing. Roads were being built; the railway line had just been extended. Such constructions were fingers rifling through the silky sediment they had disturbed, feeling the richness of the coal seams.

'*No longer will the people around here think of us as grain-scattering peasants,*' Owen would say. '*They have ideas, which they will want us to provide insurance for. Your Llew will be selling far more than is required by Tresant market. We'll have our own market here, every day.*'

Angharad was not so enthused.

Gwyn represented the here and now, with his thick-set, sturdy frame, broad more than he was tall. He had a raw energy which Angharad found alluring. They both worked at the farm that belonged to her Uncle Llewellyn. She would often observe him at work, stripped to the waist, hammering at an orange-glowing iron. Abdominal muscles pushing against the belt of his trousers. Other times she watched him in the field, digging or ploughing. He worked more than he talked; he didn't need speech, as he spoke the language of the land. He was an outdoor plant, as her Aunt Gwendolyn would say. He would not be able to spend life cooped up in an office.

In the clearing, Gwyn flung himself to the ground with abandon, scattering bees and other insects chaotically in all directions. He pulled Angharad down beside him, breaking her fall with his outstretched arm. They lay there, waiting for the rhythm of their breath to return to normal, gazing up at the spring, blue sky. Clouds of celestial breath passed by, as they were assailed by the heady aromas of the mountain. They received the blessing of the sun, which shone cheekily down on them. The gentle breeze caressed the long grass and ferns, causing them to softly sway.

Gwyn gently rolled onto his side and tenderly brushed his fingertips across Angharad's cheek. She turned towards him so she could look into the pale blueness of his eyes. Those who did not know him would describe the blue as steely and hostile. Angharad noticed the change in them, however, when he looked at the land. The times when he would place a reassuring palm against the side of a cow to steer it into the barn at the end of the day.

His powerful lips locked against hers, and her senses soared into life, made giddy by the scent exhaled from surrounding plants. She spread her fingers through his fine, sandy hair, letting it fall and flow, before moving her hand down to his chest. Her flesh-seeking fingers grappled with the cloth covering his body, restraint rapidly dissipating. Her pulsating veins felt as if they would burst.

Gwyn eagerly tore off his thick serge jacket whilst she wrestled with the buttons of his shirt. Her flesh seemed to melt as quicksand into his as her fingers dug into the blades of his shoulders, not wanting to let him go.

'Oh Gwyn, Gwyn,' she murmured softly into his neck as a powerful impulse overcame her.

Moments later, they fell back again, shamelessly looking at the sky. Fat white clouds floated slowly against a pale blue background.

'We'd better get back before they send out a search party,' said Gwyn as he sprung upright.

'Oh, stay a while longer," said Angharad serenely. 'Let's hold on to this moment for a few minutes more.'

'Sheep need to be fed and penned, as we don't want a summons from the Leet. You need to get the chickens into the coop, otherwise your Uncle Llew won't be happy if the foxes visit in the night.'

'There's a while yet before the sun goes.' Angharad made no attempt to move. 'Bopa Gwen is out visiting, so no one will know we were gone.'

'I don't trust that Taliesin at the stables, he'll tell old Llew how he was left on his own to sort out the farm.'

Angharad let out a sigh and rose resignedly to her feet. She brushed grass seeds and kernels from her skirt and clung onto Gwyn's arm as they descended back to the farm.

'Maybe we'll have a small holding ourselves one day,' Angharad said blissfully. 'We'll stay at the farm after we're married and look for some suitable dwellings nearby.'

'Hold on a minute,' Gwyn said guardedly. 'What's all this talk of marriage?'

'You mean you're not going to marry me now?' Angharad said with astonishment.

'Well, you're engaged after all. What will office boy have to say?'

'Don't tell me you're worried about him.' Angharad almost spat the words out with contempt.

'Look, just hang on a minute, shall we?'

'That's not what you were saying a minute ago.'

'I didn't mean it to happen, do you understand?'

'You could have fooled me.'

'Well, I didn't exactly notice you putting up a fight.'

'You're blaming me now!' said Angharad incredulously.

'No, I'm not blaming you. It's just that there's been something between us, and this afternoon, we were both alone, and it just happened.'

'But I want to be with you always, Gwyn. We can live on the farm when we first marry; you can move into my room whilst we look for a place to rent.'

'*Cariad.*' He put his hands on both her shoulders and looked at her with gentleness. 'How can I afford anything on a farmhand's wages?' His voice was softly imploring. 'You don't want to spend your life working on a farm. Owen can give you so much more.'

'I don't want Owen,' Angharad cried defiantly, 'I want to be with you. I don't care if we live in the pig sty.'

'You say that now,' he said bluntly, 'but give it a few years, and you'll soon be tired of all the hard work and little money. I can't let you throw away the chance you have with Owen.'

'You should have thought of that before rolling me in the clover,' Angharad said, flushing with crimson anger.

She turned and stormed back to the farm. Gwyn followed, but kept enough distance to avoid any further discussion. Back at the farm, he hurried back to his room to change, before rounding the sheep into the pens for the night.

# Chapter 8

Gaby reclined in the bath, letting the warm water cover her baptismally as she tried to let her mind go blank, to stop all the throbbing thoughts. Seeing the apparition a second time had really shaken her up. The first time could be put down to imagination, but the second could not be so easily disregarded. There was no one else she could talk to about the incident apart from Mickey, and even he was dismissive. *"Oh come on now,"* he'd said. *"Get real—all you've been talking and reading about lately is this Angharad girl. It's taken a hold of you to the extent that now you even think you're seeing her. It's your mind playing tricks on you."* She couldn't talk to other people. If they thought her strange now, they'd think she had really flipped if she said there was a girl in Victorian dress following her around.

She decided not to think about it, for the rest of the evening at least, and concentrated her mind on the immediate hours ahead of her. This was the prelude to the evening, getting ready for the night ahead. A cleansing ritual, as if preparing for some sort of spiritual initiation. She imperiously watched rivulets of condensation run down the bold, blue coloured tiles.

She enjoyed the intimate embrace of the warm water, vaguely aware in the background of the bland voices of actors in a soap opera. She examined the inside of her forearm, resting against the lip of the bath. The blue veins beneath her white skin resembled the tributaries in the atlas she had looked at as a child. That atlas had filled many an empty space in her childhood, leaving her wondering whether she would ever visit the places important enough to be printed.

Her reverie was pierced by the sound of the doorbell. *That'll be Mickey*, she thought, and rose, pink and glowing, from the soapy foam. *Time to get a move on.*

'Come in—take a seat.' Gaby's brother, Jonathan, invited Mickey into the house. 'You don't need me to tell you, she's not ready yet.'

'That's OK; I'll sit here for the next hour. Where are you off tonight?'

'Down the Colliers, mate, getting some real booze and talking about things that matter—like rugby.'

'Not that inane game.' Gaby entered the living room, robed in a dressing gown, preoccupied with looking for a brush. 'Where men put their heads forward like bulls and charge into each other. Has nothing changed since the gladiator arena?'

'It's all about tactics,' Jonathan replied playfully. 'You women don't understand.'

'Don't try and make it sound intellectual. It's just men trying to be macho, hurling themselves about on a pitch and then trying to outdrink each other. Some men can't think about anything other than sport. They've even made a sport out of sweeping floors—curling or something. What's that all about? I mean, look.' Gaby pointed towards the television. 'There's a war going on, and half the news is devoted to sport.'

'Sport is a very important part of people's lives,'

Jonathan retorted. 'I'd much rather watch sport than watch people shooting bullets at each other. Where's the skill in that? Maybe these countries should just play sport against each other, and whoever won got the country.'

'Are you seeing Cathy tonight?' Mickey interjected in an attempt to change the direction of the conversation.

'She'll probably stroll in at some point, her and her mates.'

'Must be such a privilege for her,' Gaby said derisively. 'Getting to spend a few hours with you on a Friday night.'

'You'll see her tomorrow, won't you?' Mickey leapt to his defence. 'She'll be with all the other dedicated girlfriends, watching the match from the side.'

'They don't watch the match,' Jonathan scoffed. 'They know nothing about the game; it's just an excuse for them to dress up and stand around gossiping.'

Jonathan appealed to women, with his thick, black, glossy hair. Whilst only being five foot eight, he was of an athletic build. Not the type that would attract Gaby, even if he wasn't her brother—too stereotypical. He had fallen into the machismo culture, the world of rugby and the pub, which was easily available in the locality. He had recently completed his apprenticeship as an electrician, and he intended to use his wage increase to follow the national rugby team to other countries. He had harboured dreams, as had many a local youth, of playing for the national team one day. He had even been selected for a trial, but even though he was a good player, competition was high and places few, thus relegating him to the amateur world of Saturday afternoon games and drinking copious amounts of alcohol.

Gaby sauntered into her bedroom, where she calmly put on a record, the music that would put her into a heady mood. Tonight she would mix with interesting people, a world away from the office where she worked. Socially, she did not interact very well with her work colleagues. They spoke of trivialities that mattered only in their worlds, wrapped up in tabloids and soap operas. Gaby worried she might end up like them, made bitter by monotony. A feature of their thinking was to distort the facts to fit their facetious world—the truth was dull. They had been formed by the pettiness of village life. There was safety in repetition.

Gaby had always felt a bit like an outsider. On the margins of conventional society, as if she had not adapted to the world's frequency. Even at school, she had felt apart whilst wearing the same uniform. The gossipmongers had filled in the gaps in her life that they were not party to. She had built resilience to the resentment. A resilience she wore like protective clothing.

Some of her co-workers were harmless, however. There were Mandy and Alicia, whom she would join for lunch sometimes. They led simple yet contented lives, and provided some relief to her highly charged existence.

Gaby made the final adjustment to her hair, and she was finally ready.

'Look at her,' said Jonathan, as she emerged into the living room, her hair standing stiff and upright with gel, torso draped in light cotton scarves. 'She looks like a clown.'

'I think she looks cool,' said Mickey

'Well at least I have style,' Gaby retorted to Jonathan. 'Not like you boring lot who only ever wear rugby tops and jeans.'

'Oooh, and she thinks *we* all look the same. All the Emerald crowd pose around in their weird getups, thinking how individual they are, and they all look the same. A bunch of prats.'

'Come on, Mickey, I can't stay in here any longer.'

'Enjoy the circus,' Jonathan shouted as they were leaving.

Mickey and Gaby stepped out into the pale orange light and were received by a warm, dwindling, late-spring evening, just catching the last of a vanishing day. The air was filled with the scent of warmth and Mickey's freshly shaven face. The clouds were a blur of apricot, just beginning to turn violet.

Their spirits were raised by anticipation of the weekend ahead. The routine was familiar and enjoyed by countless other youths who inhabited such villages. Public Houses had originally been put in the villages as a means of release for the miners, after a week of hard graft.

The Emerald Tree, where they were headed, was a meeting place for those who wanted more out of life. A life full of perverse possibilities in an area with a high percentage of terminal despondency. The Emerald, as it was known, had become an extension of school for many. Gaby had started going there at sixteen; very few people over twenty-five frequented the Emerald. The comprehensive school system had produced a college for yearners, comforted by tribalism.

Idealists who would plan better tomorrows. The Emerald was a place where revolutions that would never come to fruition were planned. A web of adolescent pretension, trying to bring a culture to a society where it did not exist.

The evening had gradually turned darker, hue by hue, until the shadows had died. Gaby tugged open the door of the Emerald, and the thrum of voices and harsh light spilled onto the road. Heady, expectant sounds, accompanied by snatches of music from the jukebox—confrontational, repetitive rhythms, the heartbeat of the night. The warm, thick, acrid smell of spilt beer. A surge of energy ascended through Gaby's body. This was the throbbing pulse of the village, which came to life on Friday and Saturday nights.

She made her way through the press of fragrant and hopeful bodies crammed between the faded wallpaper of the corridor, past the cigarette machine to the back room.

"Awright, Butt," a male voice acknowledged Mickey as he followed Gaby, trying to remain as close behind her as possible.

The darkness of the long, rectangular backroom hit her like a desert night after the stark, artificial glare of the entrance. Posters from avant-garde music magazines provided by regular clients decorated the whole of the ceiling, which would otherwise have been stained by tobacco smoke. An eerie beam of purple light eddied on the smoky mist circulating above their heads. The sweet tang of marijuana frolicked around their nostrils.

The end of the room was obscured by swirling smoke, through which blurred faces appeared. Chairs and tables were aligned against the walls, leaving a corridor down the middle, which was packed with bodies, as if pulled by gravity to the back room. Groups huddled around the low tables. Gaby was relieved to see her friend Maria sitting amongst other familiar faces. Maria greeted Gaby with a slight backward tilt of her head and the raising of her eyebrows.

'How's things? Have you come straight here?' asked Gaby, leaning as close to Maria as she could get.

'Nah, we called at the Labour first, left about half seven.'

The Labour was one of the social clubs, which were in every village. A residual particle of the old industrial traditions. Maria wasn't the type of outsider one would expect to frequent such institutions, but many young people did, as a stop gap before moving to more popular areas. The drinks were cheap, so they would sit in small groups, looked upon with interest by the older men, absorbed into the greyness of the walls.

Maria was bohemian, about a head shorter than Gaby and of petite build. She had been employed in a series of low-paid jobs arising out of employment schemes. She currently worked in a photography development shop, where she handled the money and dealt with basic administration. The photographer was rarely there, so she spent much of the time alone. She was only required to work about three hours each weekday, when she listened to the radio, which was permanently tuned into station one, and read magazines in between dealing with customers. Most of her clothes were bought from jumble sales or second-hand markets. She was very creative, and had cultivated a fashionable flamboyance. Gaby's mother was not fond of her, however, and felt her to be a bad influence.

'Anything happen during the week?' asked Gaby.

'Went to see Barry play at the Cedars on Wednesday. A few of us went back to the flat. Stayed up till about three. Karl was going off on one, talking about how we should all revolt.' Maria moved a cigarette to her lips.

'His usual spiel then.'

Maria's boyfriend, Barry, was unemployed. He was a drummer in a local band called the Groovy Armenian Anarchists, which got the occasional gig and dreamed about stardom. Maria and Barry had been together for about three years and shared a flat above a grocery shop.

The atmosphere was not conducive to conversation—too loud, due to the music from the jukebox and everyone else crowded into the room trying to talk. Gaby observed the other regulars, like her, revelling in the Friday night hedonism. The swagger and poise that arose from unencumbered naivety as alcohol flowed from tap to glass to mouth. Their ambitions were still dreams; they had not woken up to the reality that surrounded their unnoticed lives. Gaby did not want this present to become her future. A teacher had once told her she was destined for better things than being a shop assistant or a suburban housewife. Her mind had been made up in raw youth. Her life would have a future tense.

Gaby rejoined Mickey, who was watching the ice dance around his glass. He was standing quite a way from the jukebox, where it was somewhat quieter. Some of the other revellers stopped to talk to them when they made the difficult route to the bar or toilet.

'Oh—hi, Stevo! How's it going?' said Gaby brightly, on seeing someone she knew go past. Steven taught art at children's centres and prisons.

'I'm OK, thanks. How's things with you?'

'Still here, unfortunately. Haven't escaped yet, still working on a plan.'

'What do you want to do then? Ambassador to New York?'

'I haven't thought of that one.'

'Well do something, Gaby, for goodness' sake. Look at me—I may not get paid much, but at least I'm doing something I enjoy.'

'I'm trying to work out what I want. Meanwhile, I have the Emerald.'

'Well, you've been working at it for the past three years. Maybe it's right under your nose; you just can't see it. Anyway, I'll leave you to continue working on it, as if I don't get my round in soon, I'll be in trouble. Don't take too long, otherwise you'll be shuffling along with a walking stick still croaking about it.'

\* \* \*

Gaby and Mickey left the Emerald around ten o'clock and stepped into the crisp night air, which was bathed in an orange neon glow from the streetlights. Some of the regulars stayed until the early hours of the morning, despite the bar service being stopped at eleven o'clock.

'What are your plans for tomorrow?' asked Mickey.

'I'm going to the library tomorrow. I'll be going early though.'

'Not that murder case again'

'Yeah, I want to know more.'

'You're going to be in a strange mood tomorrow then. Why are you so obsessed with dead people when you have a live one here?'

'Keeps me out of trouble.'

'You're a strange one.' Mickey looked at her caringly. They had stopped outside her house. He kissed her gently. 'See you tomorrow outside the café, then.'

'I probably won't make it in the afternoon. I'll see you in the evening.'

They kissed each other before parting.

Gaby let herself into her dark, silent house and made her way quietly to her bedroom. She felt a contentment that she often felt after a Friday evening, a warmth as she sunk into bed and drifted off into sleep.

Within minutes, she was observing the girl from the mirror. Only this time, she was standing outside. She recognised the familiar doorframe of her grandmother's cottage, but the rest of the house and yard looked different. The walls were in need of paint, and there were the sounds of farm animals.

# Chapter 9

Angharad stood outside the door, a shawl of coarse cloth draped loosely over her shoulders. Two empty pails were held in her hands. The sun, low in the sky, tinged everything with a saffron hue. The only sounds were the joyful morning song of invisible birds, the chuckle of the magpie. The grass was damp with fresh dew, and a morning steam rose from the ground. A thin pall of smoke curled from the chimney, a result of the fire Angharad had just lit in readiness for the tasks she would undertake after tending the animals. She would let the sheep out from the pen so they could begin their day gorging on the grass from surrounding fields. They had a banquet of plenty; the grass was profuse from an abundant supply of rain. No amount of rain could make love grow, however.

Angharad morosely carried the pails to the cow shed whilst thinking of the rest of the household that would soon be rising to commence the flow of farming life. On opening the door, the pungent smell of hay and animals hit her. The deep, sonorous sound of the cows began as soon as she entered. She gently patted the tough, callous hides as she passed between them. She had a way with animals, which quickly developed into an affinity. To her, the world would be incomplete without animals.

She filled the troughs with hay and then placed

the milking stool beside the first of the bulging udders. Gently pulling on the udder in a rhythmic manner, she waited for the expectant splat of the milk hitting the bottom of the pail. This morning ritual, which she performed automatically, had a mesmerising effect, and her thoughts soon turned to Gwyn. He had been avoiding her lately. She did not understand his change in behaviour from his ardent, overpowering passion towards her during their possessive coupling that Sunday afternoon. How he had clasped her to his body, as if wanting her flesh to meld with his. How she longed to be taken into his arms once again. She had ruminated over the hours since that afternoon, trying to discover what she had done to cause this alteration in his attitude towards her. Despite meticulously analysing every moment, her thoughts revealed nothing of substance. Nothing that would elucidate the reasons for this shift in Gwyn's disposition towards her.

She had hoped the outburst after his reluctance to marry her would have settled by now. That he would have come around, taken her into his arms, soothed and reassured her that of course they will be together if that is what she really wants. Once she had been given time to consider her options, and she had chosen him, they would start to put the picture of their future together.

She felt a flutter in the base of her abdomen, and realised that she would have to talk to him soon.

She watched her fingers gently squeezing milk from the cow's udder, and noticed the ring on her finger. She thought back to Owen. His parents had owned the small grocery store in the village where she had lived. He had two older brothers and an older sister, Elizabeth. One brother worked at the mill, and the other helped run the shop. Elizabeth had gone to work as a servant for one of the estate owners.

Owen was three years older than Angharad. They had not spent much of their childhood playing together—he had mostly been with the older children. He had been kind to her, however. Once, she had fallen from a wall into someone's garden. The other children stood around laughing, watching her clumsy attempts to climb back up. Owen suddenly appeared and extended his arm to her, which she grabbed, and he pulled her to the top of the wall. He helped her to the ground, where he dusted her down.

'There, there,' he said soothingly. 'Don't cry—you'll be alright. Does it hurt anywhere?'

She tearfully lifted her skirt to just above her knees.

'Oh look,' he said. 'You've grazed your knees. We'll just go over to the stream there, and I'll clean them for you.'

He took her hand and led her to the stream, where he took a handkerchief from his pocket, which he soaked in the cool, clear water. He rung out the water and gently rubbed her knees with the damp material.

'That's better, isn't it? It looked a lot worse than it actually is. Just a few scratches. You shouldn't really be climbing other people's walls though,' he said with gentle reproval. 'You need to take care as not only could you get hurt, but the owners may be angry. Never mind, off you go home now.'

He would sometimes go to the estate owner's

house to accompany Elizabeth home on her day off. The estate owner, Mr Crawford, was rather fond of him. He would get him to talk about what went on in the village. Owen in turn would ask about steam engines—he was rather excited about a railway bridge being built in North Wales.

'Fancy Robert Stephenson building a bridge in Wales,' he would say, eyes bright and wide. 'I wonder if he will build one here?'

Mr Crawford had always been impressed by Owen's intelligence. Elizabeth would relay his comments back to her mother, who in turn would try to persuade his father to send him to the school at Tresant.

'We can't afford that!' his father had said. 'We have enough to do making ends meet as it is. It's not only the fees—there are the clothes he would need, and the travel.'

His mother got the three other children to agree to help with the money, however, until his father finally relented.

Owen had often called and seen Angharad on the weekends, when he was not at school. She had not particularly relished these visits, but it became a habit. Her parents, however, encouraged the relationship.

'Oooh, that Owen is such a nice boy,' her mother would gush, 'and he looks so smart in his school clothes. He's growing into a nice young gentleman.'

He commenced work as an apprentice at the insurance company in the nearby town. He started to take Angharad out and buy her nice things. They got engaged before she started at the farm. She accepted his proposal, as it was the thing to do. She would have to marry someone someday, so why not Owen?

Then, at the farm, she had met Gwyn. She remembered being introduced to him.

"This is our Gwyn," said her aunt Gwendolyn. "Doesn't say much, but he's a hard working boyo, is our Gwyn."

He inclined his head barely perceptibly towards her, and she gave a small smile. Her aunt pointed out the rest of the farm, but Angharad struggled with the urge not to stare at Gwyn. The sight of him had struck her with a force she had never felt before. *So this is what it is like to be in love,* she thought

The final cow had been milked, so her next task was to feed the chickens.

They ran clucking towards her at the sight of the pail full of corn. She watched them pecking at the particles she had scattered to the ground. Soon there would be the customary sounds of the household going about its business, and so would begin her battle against the dust and debris of the previous day, the restoration of cleanliness and order. *"Cleanliness is next to godliness,"* her aunt would often say.

Angharad collected the eggs that she would prepare for breakfast; hopefully she would have the chance to talk to Gwyn before he started his labours. Today was market day at Tresant. He would pile the hefty sacks of oat and wheat onto the cart, and both he and Taliesin would set off after breakfast and return just before darkness. Angharad would spend much of the evening worrying and listening for the rattle of the cartwheels over the stone. Many a cart had been overturned on the ridgeway route.

Gwendolen was briskly moving around the scullery when Angharad entered.

'*Bore Da*, Angharad. What's it like out there?'

'Another fine day, Bopa.'

'Then we'd better get cracking. These men will be up soon for market.'

'I'd better get this hot water to the bowls, then.'

Angharad unhinged the large pot hanging over the fire and tipped some water into a metal bowl, which she took into the washroom, and waited for Gwyn.

'What are you doing here?' Gwyn said abruptly, his expression quickly turning into a brooding scowl.

'Waiting for you, as you've been avoiding me these past weeks.'

'It's hard graft round here, init.'

'Nothing's changed around here, apart from you.'

'Why are you nagging me?' Angharad winced with each slash of his razor against the sharpening strap.

'I think I'm with child,'

'JESUS!' exclaimed Gwyn, astounded. 'Have you told Owen?'

'What's it to do with him?'

'You're engaged to him for goodness' sake. You'd better marry him quick.'

'I don't want to marry Owen—I want to marry you,' Angharad said pleadingly.

'I've told you, there's no money to be made in farming,' Gwyn said obstinately.

'I don't care about money. I just want to be with you.'

'What life is that for a child?' said Gwyn with

controlled mildness. He turned to face her and placed his hands placatingly on her shoulders. 'Grow up on a farm, die on a farm. Owen can give you so much more.'

'I don't want what Owen can give.' Salt stung Angharad's eyes. 'I want you.'

'If you can't think of yourself, think of the child,' Gwyn said briskly.

'Do something else,' Angharad entreated. 'Owen says there's a future here. People with money will be wanting to buy coal.'

'Farming's a way of life. It's in my blood,' Gwyn said stubbornly.

'What's good enough for you is good enough for your child.'

'Oh, you're not listening, woman.' Gwyn plunged his hands into the bowl of water with exasperation. 'You're as stubborn as the mules I have to clod.'

Gwyn strode out of the washroom, leaving Angharad to return to the scullery and assist Gwendolyn in the preparation of breakfast.

# Chapter 10

There was only one thing on Gaby's mind that morning, and she was impatient to start the day. Since the vision in the mirror, the murder case had never been far from her mind in one way or another. She was either wondering why the apparition had appeared to her—was the girl trying to tell her something? Otherwise, she was questioning her sanity.

Nevertheless, her life seemed to have taken on a new meaning since the incident. There was a drive to find out more about the case. Mickey couldn't understand where she got the energy from. It was a compulsion to find out more and more, as if she was being driven by some unseen force.

On Saturday mornings, she normally loitered around and made the most of not being in abeyance to the alarm clock. Today, however, she was washed, dressed and eager to get to the library. She grabbed her jacket and headed out the door whilst still consuming the last of her breakfast.

'Got a bus to catch?' her father shouted indignantly from the living room.

'Oh! Bye, Dad! Bye, Mam!' She shouted back before closing the door.

She reached the library in record time, even though it was over a mile from her parents' home. The librarian gave a nod of familiar acknowledgement as Gaby headed straight to the archives. She knew exactly where to find the news records and quickly found the microfiche containing the newspaper from the date she was looking for. She placed the slide in the machine and adjusted the focus so she could read the headline.

*MAN ARRESTED IN CONNECTION WITH TY COCH MURDER*

*A man is being held in connection with the death of Angharad Morgan, who was found in the early hours of the morning of Monday 9 June with her throat slashed to the point of being severed from her body. The man in question, Owen Thomas, is believed to have been the fiancé of the victim. The inquest has recorded death by wilful murder, and the case is to be heard by the Magistrates' Court at Tarfarn Newydd, Monday 30 June, 1862.*

Gaby went back to the index cards, hasty fingers rifling through the pack, rapidly finding Tuesday 1 July, 1862. She read that the benches were filled to overflowing and the anticipation was palpable from the crowd gathered to hear the case against Owen Thomas, for the murder of Angharad Morgan.

Llewellyn Morgan was called on to give evidence and the following extract of his evidence was given:

*He had left Ty Coch around four o'clock to go to the Tafarn Seren, which he left around twenty minutes to six in order to attend the evening chapel service at six o'clock. He was surprised that his niece Angharad was not there. He had a fleeting glimpse of her fiancé, Owen, leaving at the end of the service. He arrived back at Ty Coch around half past seven, where he informed his wife, Gwen, that Angharad had not been at the service. Gwen expressed surprise, as Angharad had left around half past five, saying she was to meet Owen for Chapel. Gwen said they had probably decided to go somewhere else—after all, they had much to discuss with their impending wedding.*

*They had settled down for the evening when there was a knock on the door. This must have been around eight o'clock. Llewellyn was surprised to see Owen at the door in an agitated state. He said Angharad had not turned up to meet him at their usual place. He had been looking everywhere for her; he had been to the chapel, but she was not there. Gwen informed him she had left around half past five saying she was to meet him. A look of concern came over his face, and he went off muttering something about Angharad seeing another man.*

The next person to give evidence was Gwyn Evans, who was employed at the farm by Llewellyn Morgan. Gwyn described how he had left Ty Coch not long after Llewellyn to go to the Tafarn Seren. He stopped at the house of his friend Idris Lewis on the way, to wash some blood from his face after accidently cutting himself with some shears that day. This incident was later confirmed by the stable boy, Taliesin. He left for the Seren around half past four with Idris.

Iestyn Rowlands, a friend of Owen, gave evidence in which he confirmed he had met Owen, who arrived at the Seren around five o'clock. Iestyn testified that Owen seemed to be in a vexed mood on arrival and was drinking more heavily than usual.

The intensity of concentration was making Gaby feel giddy. Thoughts swirled around her head. She was in a whirlpool of blackness, eddying and swaying out of control. She looked for something around her on which to anchor her mind, but everything was out of focus and there was nothing coherent which she could use. Amongst the rush of walls and objects moving around her, with much effort, she fixed her thoughts on a sepia photograph hanging on an opposite wall. The photograph seemed to get closer and closer, until she found herself in the picture itself—sitting on a wooden bench, wedged amongst a crowd, gazing raptly at a court scene.

There were long tables, formed by smaller tables put together, the surfaces of which were stained with glutinous rings.

'Can you tell the court the conversation that took place between you and the accused at the Tafarn Seren on the evening of Sunday the eighth of June?'

'He was talking about how things were going to change around here. "There's wealth beneath this earth, Iestyn," he said. "Well," I said, "I could do with some of it." "It's there for the taking," he replied, but he never looked at me, he kept staring straight ahead, whilst taking gulps of ale between talking.

'"Don't know if this place will be here in two years' time," he went on. "Well," I said, "I'll need some bloody place to have a drink." "Oh, there'll be places, all right," he said. "But not as you and I know them."

'This serious talk was starting to make me feel uncomfortable. "Hadn't you better get going if you're to meet Angharad?" I said. His face went kind of numb-like. "I may as well be one of the cows she milks, for all the interest she seems to take of me lately," he says. "Well, maybe she's getting a bit nervous about the wedding, you know like," I said. "Things like this are big for women. Although, she hasn't got much to worry about, after all, she's not going to want for much."

"'Fat lot of good that seems to be doing," he replied. "All the hard work I've put in, trying to get things together to create a good life for us, and all she seems to want to do is to spend time hanging around that oaf of a farm worker." He nods his head towards Gwyn Evans, who was sitting over by the wall with Idris Lewis.

"'Hang on a minute, Owen," I said. "You don't know that for sure. After all, it's hard work on the farm, and it's not exactly a massive bit of land. They can hardly avoid each other." With that, he drained the last of his ale and said, "I best be off then. I may call at your Mam's next Wednesday." We said our goodbyes, and off he went.'

'What time would this have been?'

'It was twenty-five minutes to six.'

'Are you quite sure of that?'

'Oh yes.'

'How can you be so sure?'

'As I heard the train go past that passes the Seren every Sunday at twenty-five minutes to six.'

Gaby shifted in her seat a little, as it was uncomfortable sitting on something so unyielding and being pressed by bodies on either side.

'The defence now calls upon Idris Lewis as the next witness.'

After swearing on the Bible, Idris explained

how he was a friend of Gwyn Evans, who had called around his house around ten minutes past four. He asked if he could have a handkerchief to wipe some dried blood from his face. He said he had cut himself whilst sharpening a shears that day.

'I said to him, maybe it's the Lord's way of telling you not to work on a day he's deemed a day of rest. "Work never stops on a farm," he says. We then walked to the Seren, which we reached at about quarter to five, where we had a mug of ale.'

'How did his mood seem at this time? Did you notice anything different about his manner?'

'No, he was his usual, same self.'

'Did he seem anxious at all?'

'No. Difficult to tell with Gwyn, keeps hisself to hisself. I did notice one thing however. Oh, it's probably nothing,' he said dismissively.

'Please, Mr Lewis, it is important that you state every detail, however inconsequential it may seem.'

'Well, he didn't seem to look at me much whilst we were drinking. Just stared straight ahead, distant-like, even when talking to me. He's never been one to show his feelings, Gwyn. He does throw me the odd glance now and again though. But that evening, he never looked at me much at all.'

'What did you talk about?'

'Oh, this and that. How things were going on the farm, the owner Llew and his wife Gwen. I asked about Angharad—he was never one for the ladies, Gwyn. Couldn't seem to relate to them, but he'd seemed to be spending more time with her lately. It was then his face became cold. "She used to be fun," he says, "but now all she does is nag. What is it with women? They have to turn into such a burden." With that, he gets up, says, "I'll be on my way then", thanks me for letting him wash the blood from his face, and went off. This would have been around fifteen minutes past five, which was earlier than he usually leaves, but I was glad, as he was in such a sullen mood.'

The magistrate then called upon Llewellyn Morgan to give evidence.

'I went to the chapel service at six o'clock and was surprised not to see Angharad there. I said so to my wife, Gwen, when I got home about half past seven. She was also surprised, as she said Angharad had left at about half past five to meet Owen for Chapel. I said I had looked around for her at the end of the service and was sure I saw Owen leaving on his own. We did say "What have those two got up to now." I said, "Maybe they've run off to get married", to which Gwen said, "They won't get far without a minister."'

'About eight o'clock there's a knock on the door, and it was Owen, wanting to know if Angharad was there. He said he'd been due to meet Angharad twenty to six at the bottom of the track, he was late and had got there about ten minutes to six, and she was not there. He thought she must have been angry and gone to Chapel without him. He slipped into the back of the chapel, saw she was not there, so waited until the end and rushed out to look for her.'

'How did he seem at this time?'

'Well, he was a bit shaken up, obviously, and then Gwen told him Angharad had left about half past five to go to Chapel. Well, he looked really concerned then and went off muttering about Angharad seeing another man! Gwen and I, we just looked at each other, and Gwen remarked that Angharad had been acting somewhat strange these past few weeks, what with moping about, crying and looking unwell.'

'Where was Gwyn Evans at this time?'

'I dunno—I never thought about it. I assumed he was either in bed or down the Seren.'

'Please continue, Mr Morgan.'

'Well, I ran after Owen and told him to try Megan Williams, and if Angharad wasn't there, she'd probably gone to her Mam's. Her mother lives three miles away, so it was a fair trek. I hoped she wasn't there, as she wouldn't be back in time to milk the cows the next day.

'Owen goes off to look some more, and I go to bed. Next thing, my wife is shaking me, all worried-like, as it was eleven o'clock and there was no sign of Angharad. I said she'd probably gone to her Mam's, but Gwen said she wouldn't do that and neglect her duties. She insists me and Gwyn go looking, so I wake Gwyn and we go looking high and low all over the farm to no avail. So we puts our heads together and decide what is the route she was most likely to take to the chapel. We decided the shortest route, so that's where we started. We took the lamp, but thankfully the moon was bright, so we could see our way, but we were none too happy, both of us cursing at how inconsiderate she was. We were both shouting her name, then all of a sudden we froze. There was Angharad's body, lying still on the floor. We rushed over to her, I shook her, and to my horror, her head practically fell away from her shoulders.

'I could hear Gwyn shouting *No!* behind me. I put my arm around his shoulders and turned him away from the body, as I could see he was in terrible shock, like. I said, "There's been a terrible accident, and we'd better get P.C Griffiths out".

'On the way to P.C Griffiths, we passed Gwyn's friend Idris's house, so I knocked on the door, explained there had been a terrible accident, and asked if he had any brandy for Gwyn. I felt it best to leave Gwyn with Idris and went on to P.C Griffiths.'

The magistrate then called upon P.C Griffiths to give evidence.

'I was woken in the early hours by a knocking on my door. I looked at the clock and it was ten past one! I thought, *Who on earth can be knocking at this hour?* I was not well pleased, as you can imagine. I opened the door, ready to give someone a piece of my mind, and there was Llew Morgan looking as if he'd just seen a ghost. Pale as a sheet, he was. "What's happened, Llew?" I said. "Oh, P.C Griffiths, you must come quick," he says. "Something terrible has happened. Angharad is dead." "Dead!" I say in disbelief. "How?"

'He starts gushing on nineteen to the dozen about how she was due to meet her fiancé and hadn't turned up for chapel. When she hadn't come home at eleven o'clock, he and Gwyn the farm worker went searching and found her on the short track with her head cut off. He said she must have fallen on a rock and cut her neck.

'He led me to the body, and when we got there, I couldn't believe my eyes. She was lying on the ground, deathly white, so I bent close to see her with the light of my bullseye. Her throat had been cut from ear to ear, and her head was at such an angle as to be practically severed from her shoulders. Her clothes were covered in blood, and her bonnet was about four feet away. I examined the bonnet, and the ribbon was saturated in blood and cut in two. Then I noticed a razor near the bonnet, and something did strike me as strange. There was a brooch—a round brooch of rubies—and I thought to myself, *Why take off the brooch and leave it by the side of the body?*

'I said to Llew, "Come on, Llew. We'd best get you home." I showed him the razor, however, and asked if he'd seen it before. He said, "That looks like Gwyn's." I said, "Let's go and compare them."

'When we get to the farm, Gwen rushes out to us, so we have to sit her down and tell her what had happened. Most difficult thing I have ever had to do in my life, Your Honour. After we'd settled her and given her a cup of tea, we went to the cupboard where Gwyn keeps his razor, but it was not there. I looked at the razor in my possession again, and the strange thing was, examining it by the light of the farm lamps, there was not a trace of blood on either the blade or handle.'

# Chapter 11

The coroner gave the result of the post mortem, in which he placed the time of death as between six o'clock and seven o'clock. He then disclosed that Angharad had been with child at the time of her death, which elicited gasps from the public gallery, accompanied by much murmuring.

Both Gwyn and Owen, who were now suspects in the case, were questioned. Gaby was surprised by how large Gwyn was. He was not tall, about five foot nine, but bulky. She could understand why women would find him attractive, in a hunky sort of way. Blond hair and blue eyes weren't common around these parts, so he would definitely have stood out.

Owen, on the other hand, was very dapper. Gaby could not take her eyes off him. *Why would anyone in their right mind choose Gwyn over him?* she thought. He obviously took pride in his appearance—immaculate, articulate.

Gwyn had left the Seren at fifteen minutes past five for Chapel, as he intended taking the long route to avoid Owen and Angharad, who were accustomed to taking the short route. He left the chapel at the end of the service and took the long route straight back to the farm and went to bed. He admitted he and Angharad had been lovers, and that he cared about her but had no desire to marry her and wanted out. She had been a nuisance around this time, but he certainly did not want her dead. There was no trace of blood on the clothes he had been wearing, which had been examined by police and doctors, apart from a small amount on the collar, which he explained was sustained through sharpening shears.

Owen got to the bottom of the track of the short route at ten minutes to six, which was a little late, as he had arranged to meet Angharad at twenty minutes to six, and after hanging around for five minutes, he thought she must have been angry and had made her way to the chapel. He therefore ran most of the way up the short track and reached the chapel about ten minutes past six, where he surreptitiously took a seat near the entrance, behind the congregation. The minister confirmed his late arrival, as he made it his duty to remember unpunctuality in his flock, which he regarded as an insult to the Lord. Owen was surprised that Angharad was not at the chapel, so at the end of the service sought to look for her, taking the long route, as he had already seen the short route.

The magistrate for the prosecution, Justice Price, pointed out that the blood on the bonnet suggested Angharad had been wearing it at the time her throat was cut. How, then, had it got to be so far from the body? Either the bonnet had been removed, or the body had been moved. The coroner confirmed it would be well-nigh impossible for any person moving the bonnet or the body not to have had noticeable traces of blood on their clothes.

Justice Price enquired whether the deceased could have crawled from where her body lay.

'Pretty damn difficult with your head hanging

off your body,' was the coroner's response, which resulted in some suppressed laughter from the gallery.

There were no signs of dirt over the body and the clothes were not in disarray, which one would expect from someone crawling with such an injury, even if attempting to move after the first cut.

With no traces of blood on the clothing of either of the accused, the defence counsel turned to the razor belonging to Gwyn Evans as the murder weapon. There was no blood on the razor either, and even if Gwyn had managed to wipe all traces of blood from the razor, why would he have left it at the scene, thus implicating himself as the assailant?

Owen appeared distraught on the witness stand. He broke down when explaining how Angharad and he had been planning their future together. How, on finding Angharad was not at their usual meeting place, he had rushed to the chapel, quietly slipped onto the back bench so as not to be noticed. He had looked around for Angharad, and on not seeing her, had thought she must have been angry with him and had returned to the cottage.

Justice Price slowly paced before the witness stand, face serious with concentration.

'Did you know the deceased was with child on the evening of Sunday the eighth of June?' he addressed Owen gravely.

'No.' Owen's eyes glistened with tears.

'Had you carnal knowledge of the deceased?'

'No.'

'So the child was obviously not yours.'

Owen kept staring fixedly ahead.

'I put it to you, Mr Thomas, that you did know your fiancée was pregnant by another man. You had suspected that she was seeing another man. You had planned to meet her at twenty minutes to six on the evening of Sunday the eighth of June with the sole intention of killing her. When the deed had been accomplished, you realised the enormity of your crime and tried to act as normally as possible. You attended the chapel service as you had done every previous Sunday. When the service had ended, you called at the home of your fiancée, took a razor belonging to Gwyn Evans and returned to the scene of the crime, where you placed the razor in order that blame be cast on Mr Evans.'

'*That's not true!*' Owen shouted out fervently. 'I loved her; we were to be married.'

'Maybe, but she did not feel the same about you.'

Owens's head dropped to his chest.

'Fifteen minutes until closing time.'

Gaby was jarred back to the stark, electric light and surrounding functional library shelves. She struggled to regain her composure. The library was closing soon—it was imperative that she found the verdict of the case. Her body was sluggish due to lack of movement, and refused to respond as she willed her reluctant muscles into action.

She vigorously skimmed the news pages on the microfiche, impatiently forcing each slide into the viewing tray, in the urgent way she'd feed coins into a public telephone as it warned her that her call time was ending.

The print fell across the screen like a waterfall,

which suddenly froze as if invaded by an ice age. Gaby's jaw went slack, her eyes stuck to the screen, expression suspended with incredulity. The headline in front of her seemed to fill the screen.

*DEATH BY SUICIDE*

She could not believe what she had just read, so read the line again, as if rereading would make the words more comprehensible or change the meaning.

The voice of the librarian broke into her fixated thoughts.

'Closing time.'

# Chapter 12

The bright sunshine hit Gaby like a slap as soon as she stepped outside from the library onto the street. She was light-headed and overwhelmed from the past hour. The blast of sunshine and thoughts swirling around her head churned up sensations of throbbing queasiness and disorientation.

She staggered across the library car park and headed instinctively towards the bus stop, guided by the barely registered sounds of traffic and people going about their Saturday afternoon rituals. She stepped off the bus as if automatically programmed and found herself at the zone where the buildings ended and nature began. She knew she was on Brynhalig Mountain, but could not remember getting here. It was as if she had sleep-walked. She vaguely recalled people, pavements and trees rushing past her. Her feet being one of many pairs stopped at traffic lights, as if part of a dream.

An ease gradually took control, her thoughts slackened, the beat of her pulse became less urgent. A cool down, like an athlete would undertake after strenuous exercise.

Fortunately, there were not too many people around, just a few, enjoying the world of late spring on a Saturday afternoon. Gaby lay back in the grass, letting the soothing sensation console her. The sky was a generous blue lid above her.

The weather was too warm for this time of year. More like a summer's day.

There was an ancient Celtic well near here, a medieval shrine. The well was said to have healing powers, and attracted pilgrimages even to this day. Many such tracts of land had been turned into places of religious devotion.

Maybe the essence of the earth had been perceived, as a hospital had also been built nearby. It was founded in the early 1900s to deal with a smallpox outbreak. The disease had been rife in the area at that time, due to the unsanitary conditions brought about by overpopulation and unsuitable accommodation. Another by-product of the mining industry.

Gaby felt the tension being drawn from her, as if by a soft, magnetic force. Melting into the earth beneath her, pinning her to the ground like some Gullivian character. Compelling her to release the tightness of her mind, until the last of the frenzied thoughts subsided into tranquillity. Questions arising from the afternoon's deliberations drifted through her mind, but the questions were now less demanding.

There were no signs that Angharad had struggled, suggesting she must have known her assailant. Why was Gwyn so unconcerned that Angharad had not been at the Church service that evening, if he had cared about her as much as he had pleaded on the witness stand? Why hadn't he enquired as to her whereabouts, on reaching the cottage and not finding her there? Instead, he had gone straight to bed! Angharad's demands on him were becoming oppressive.

The weapon that killed her was his razor. He

was not clever like Owen, but it would have been so fatuous to have left the murder weapon at the scene of the crime. He had left the Seren at quarter past five, according to Idris, and took the long route to the chapel, where he arrived at six. Idris confirmed this was earlier than he usually left. Why? Was this because he was taking the long route? Was this just to avoid Angharad and Owen, as he had given as the reason? How long would the long route take? Forty five minutes seemed a long time. Had anyone seen him during this time? Which route had he really taken back to the farm? Whoever had killed Angharad had done so in such a manner that they would surely have been covered in blood. Could Gwyn have disposed of his clothes somehow? Gwen had confirmed the clothes he was wearing were the ones he had given to the police. There were scratches on his neck, which the stable boy had confirmed he had seen being sustained by sharpening a shears. Could Gwyn have bribed or threatened the stable boy?

Gaby turned her attention to Owen. The lover was usually high on the list of suspects in such cases. Could this have been a crime of passion? Iestyn had noticed Owen's growing resentment and anger building up over the increasing amount of time Angharad seemed to be spending at the farm rather than with him. Owen had left the Seren at five thirty-five—his alibi had been quite sure of that. There would have been a ten minute walk to the spot where he had arranged to meet Angharad—this would be around five forty-five. He waited five minutes then rushed to Chapel, where he asserted, and it was confirmed by the minister, that he had arrived about ten minutes after the service had commenced.

This would correspond with his testimony, as the walk from the bottom of the track took around twenty minutes, so by rushing, it was feasible that Owen could have reached his destination in fifteen minutes or less. That would put both Gwyn and Owen away from the victim at the time of death.

Angharad's body had been found halfway down the track. Even though Owen had been close to the area, there would have been insufficient time to have inflicted the killing blow and to have changed and hidden his clothes within the time it took to reach the chapel.

Why did he rush out after the service? Surely it would have made more sense, on seeing that Angharad was not amongst the congregation, to have approached Llewellyn to ascertain whether he had any idea of when Angharad had left the farm. Why, also, take the long path back? If he'd thought she might be at the farm, wouldn't it have been more logical to take the shortest route back to the farm and check there before searching the long route? The reason he gave in his testimony was that he had already seen the short route. This explanation seemed a little too convenient, somehow.

A verdict of *suicide*! How on earth was it possible for someone to sever their own head from their body with a razor? Imagine the strength it would take another person to do so, let alone a young female.

'What was wrong with you people?' Gaby heard herself shriek, before closing her eyes due to the demands of her exertion.

The next sensation she became aware of was of a soft fabric being gently stroked across her brow. She opened her eyes, and there was the girl from the mirror, looking back at her with an expression of compassion and concern.

'What do you want from me?' Gaby exclaimed loudly and sat bolt upright.

The vision before her slowly faded, whilst keeping the same concerned expression fixed on Gaby.

'I don't know what it is you want,' Gaby said wearily, whilst using one hand to push herself onto her feet.

She felt fragile, and bewilderingly made her way back to the cottage.

'Oh! What has happened to you, *merched*?' her grandmother said with anguish on seeing Gaby stagger through the door.

Gaby glared challengingly at her grandmother. '*What are you hiding from me*?'

# Chapter 13

Angharad forced her cumbersome legs, heavy with reluctance, up the well-trodden mountain track towards the chapel. She did not want to go, but her absence would only solidify suspicion.

Owen was waiting for her in the usual place. She weakly returned his smile and took his arm so he could accompany her on their way towards the accusing sound of the bell. She tried to avoid the affection in his eyes. Affection that she longed to see reflected back from Gwyn's eyes.

The sun was bright, although no longer in the middle of the sky. She was grateful for the tall hedges either side of her, but then they reached the end of the track and were out in the open, exposed part of the mountainside. The mountain levelled here, providing a ledge of flatness, before ascending again to the steep summit.

The only sound that could be heard was the full bellow of the bell, commanding attendance. The stone chapel rose out of the greenery. A simple building, larger than the farm cottage and many other houses in the village but made small by the surrounding expanse.

Little tufts of ferns poked through the low wall surrounding the chapel. Some villagers had gathered at the narrow gate. This was the access point, where they were made to hesitate, so greetings had become a necessary custom. Angharad could not hear the commonplace, irrelevant chatter from this distance, however; the bell was the loudest voice of all.

An anxious atmosphere descended upon the crowd on entering the small, sacred building. Solemnity was an essential characteristic in this place of worship, bringing morality and restraint to the community, teaching responsibility to fellowmen. The only ornamentation was a picture of Jesus, hung high on the wall, looking over the congregation with a smile that knew their sins. Light from narrow windows challenged the dimness. Villagers sat closely together on long, solid, wooden benches, feet placed flatly and firmly on the scrubbed stone floor.

Angharad fastened her steely gaze on the wall in front of her, the pressure of being in this sancti-monious chamber becoming claustrophobic. There was a queasy, unsettling feeling in the pit of her stomach. Soft limbs formed in her rounding abdo-men, a ripening fruit that would need to be released.

Much effort was required to focus straight ahead. To avoid the eyes she sensed were drawn to her with a magnetic force. A force burning into her, branding her. Were they aware of her emerging swell? She had heard the whispers and accusations drifting through the small window whilst she swept the scullery floor. Gossips of the village, reaching their own conclusions, giving evidence to their own claims. She had broken a social code. Committed an offence against society. Society's laws, but not nature's laws.

The unease became palpable. Awaiting with apprehension the minister's footsteps down the silent aisle. Ascending the steps to the raised pulpit, fearing his menacing gaze. Men three times larger than he would shrink from that gaze. Any other being who would dare to hurl such insults at them as flowed from the minister's condemning tongue would be knocked to the ground by a clenched, brawny fist.

The minister made his entrance, moving slowly down the aisle as if through a parting sea, black book clutched tightly to his chest. Heads bowed in deferential fear as he walked past each pew. He looked down at the congregation before him. A long, scrawny body, the yellow pallor of his face accentuated by his worn, black suit. Eyes stern, protruding. A voice hard with the distaste that grows from years of condemning and accusing, assuming people are sinful. The result of a sense of superiority that arises from being chosen by God.

A sombre strain of chords from the organ announced the commencement of the first hymn. The small hall was filled with the congregation's mingled voices, resonating from wall to wall. The hymn ended, and the minister fixed his harsh, austere glare on his obedient, servile audience. A look from which no one was spared, making them feel exposed, as if he had some God-given insight into their thoughts.

He began his address softly, but it was a cold, formidable softness. Stillness fell over the small crowded hall. The suspension that happens before a disturbance to the natural order, such as a turbulent storm or an earthquake. A diversion that nature could sense.

'So we gather here today to praise God. God, who gave his only son to the world, in order that we can be saved from sin.

'Do you deserve such a gracious saviour?' His mouth twisted around the words, voice thick with disdain, cold eyes surveying each of the congregation. No one escaped the frosty, penetrating glare as it alighted on a chosen face. Trapped, like a rabbit by a surrounding pack of hounds.

'Does it mean anything to you?' His voice became louder, preparing for the launch. 'I think not.' He stopped there, like a cruel tormentor, to savour the unease he had created. 'For I look around me.' He paused to gauge the reaction. The crowd did not dare to avert their gaze. 'I see the drunken squalor of the evenings.' Voice now powerful, the sinews of his neck strained. 'I hear the loud laughter and frivolity, seeping through the walls of the Seren. That temple to the devil. I see the bodies staggering out of its doors, lurching your way back to your homes at night.' Another interlude of guilty silence. 'Don't think the darkness can hide your sins.'

Now came the blow.

'For God can see into each and every one of your souls. He knows your dark, evil thoughts. He gave you guidance.' He thrust the black book above him, his right arm fully extended. 'But you turn away. Treating his word with disdain.'

He allowed this message to sink in before returning to the book on the pedestal before him. 'I read from Galatians.'

The congregation had a few seconds respite whilst he turned the pages.

'Works of the flesh are plain.' His voice was now booming. 'Fornication, idolatry, sodomy, drunkenness, carousing and the like. I warn you, as I warned you before.' The frenzied voice now rose to a crescendo.

Angharad tasted the dryness of her mouth. Pulse throbbing, *He knows*, she thought. *He sees my sins. I cannot hide; I may as well be naked before him.*

The rest of the sermon became a drone of words. She jumped at the hammer of the minister's fist as it smashed down on the Bible. The pounding of her heart made all understanding futile.

Angharad used an empty patch of wall alongside the minister as an anchor to stay afloat, to avoid becoming engulfed by her imagined condemnation. The final hymn eventually came. The last, long, drawn out "Amen" from Owen's, strong, sonorous voice caused her shoulders to relax with relief.

The minister, voice now returned to how it had been at the beginning of the service, gave the blessing and reminded everybody to walk in the grace of God during the coming week. With the effort of a smile, he dismounted the small platform and led the way down the aisle, accompanied by music from the organ. The first pew followed, the others joining systematically as the last person passed, with the precision of a clockwork toy.

Angharad clung to Owen's arm, trying to avoid the accusing eyes waiting at the end of each pew she passed on her way down the interminable aisle. She dared not glance towards the seat Gwyn usually took, although it took great restraint not to do so.

On stepping through the door, she felt the pressure release like the escape of steam from a condensed container once the cap had been unscrewed. The light, early-summer air was comforting, but there was the formality of making small talk with the rest of the congregation. Another small rite before the final escape.

Ethel Roberts glanced toward her with malevolence. Ethel, tall and magisterial, was dressed in fine threads, lace billowing between the openings of her small jacket. Parasol balanced delicately on her shoulder, her hand lightly rested on her husband Lloyd's forearm. Lloyd was a large man, not overweight, but tall and broad chested. He had thick black hair, which he smoothed flat with oil down either side of his middle parting, and a black moustache, the ends of which he twirled with wax. One eye was monocled, and a heavy gold watch chain always hung from his waistcoat pocket. He was genial and ebullient.

'Hello, Angharad,' came Mrs Robert's genteel but slightly caustic voice. 'How are things on the farm these days?'

Angharad felt herself become rigid, every muscle taut. 'Very busy at the moment, thank you, Mrs Roberts.'

'You have Gwyn to help you.' Angharad detected a slight, sardonic smile.

'He has his own work to do,' Angharad replied frostily.

'Oh, come now,' Mrs Roberts proclaimed superciliously. 'Surely he does not allow you to drudge away? After all, he is very fond of you.'

'You know how it is at this time of the year, Mrs Roberts,' Angharad replied stiffly. 'Sheep need shearing, crops need watering. Life can be harsh up in the mountain.'

'Well, things will change when you and Owen wed.'

'Things will be better for everyone around here soon,' Owen interjected with certainty.

'Only God can do anything about the seasons.' Lloyd Roberts voice was loud and cheerful. 'Man cannot do anything about the sun and rain the farm workers rely on.'

'Maybe so, Mr Roberts,' Owen replied curtly, 'but God has put a lot here for man which he's only just discovered.'

'Oh yes,' enthused Mrs Roberts. 'We are surrounded by such beauty. A constant reminder of God's grace and wonder.'

'There's more to God's abundance than can be seen with the eye, Mrs Roberts,' Owen said assuredly.

'Oh that I know. God's grace is infinite, despite the sin he sees.' Mrs Roberts cast a disdainful look towards Angharad.

'I don't think that is what Owen means, my dear.' a smile played under Mr Roberts' moustache, amused by the naivety and idealism of youth. 'Man's greed wants to turn all of nature's good that you see about you into profit.'

'Isn't that what God put the fruits of the earth here for, Mr Roberts?' Owen said challengingly. He locked his blazing eyes onto those of Mr Roberts as if confronting an opponent in a boxing match. 'Fruit was put on trees for man to eat, and beasts of burden to do our work.'

'Aye, and look what happened when man picked the fruit off the tree. That's when everything fell into chaos. That's what happens when you listen to a woman, see.' Mr Roberts gave a playful wink towards Angharad.

'And why shouldn't people around here benefit from God's provisions?' Owen argued belligerently. 'Goodness knows they've worked hard enough, whilst the land-owning classes have got rich on the rents from these lands. Living out of sight on their estates.' Owen stared defiantly at Lloyd Roberts.

'I fear it won't be the likes of workers around here who will benefit, Owen my lad. Why, here's Daffydd the Siop.' Lloyd Roberts used the convenience of this appearance. 'How's trade with you these days?'

'Oh, better since they've built the railroad see.'

'And how are you, Mrs Griffiths?' Lloyd Roberts turned his attention to the lady accompanying Daffydd. 'I hope he is treating you well, with the betterments of his trade.'

'I can't complain,' replied Olwyn Griffiths. 'Nice to see you in good spirits as always, Mr Roberts, and good to see you too, Ethel. Owen and Angharad, I haven't seen you two about for a long time. Keeping ourselves hidden are we?'

'As I was explaining to Mrs Roberts earlier,' said Angharad hastily, 'there's much to do on the farm at present.'

'And as I pointed out,' Ethel Roberts quickly returned, 'she has that big, strong lad Gwyn to help.'

'Oh yes, Gwyn,' said Olwyn Griffiths, as if the thought had only just been put in her mind. 'He came into the shop the other day to have his razor sharpened, looking as sullen as the day is long. He could do with reading his Bible more often.'

'Well, we best be going,' Owen said with as much civility as he could muster. 'After all,

Angharad needs her sleep, to deal with all the work the farm requires.'

'Yes, she certainly needs that,' Ethel Roberts cynically agreed.

Owen and Angharad walked off arm in arm, under the watchful gaze of both couples.

'He's got fire in him, that one,' Lloyd Roberts said affectionately. 'I wonder how long it will take for that to burn less bright.'

'I don't know what he sees in that insipid peasant girl,' said Ethel Roberts with a touch of animosity.

'Oh, she's got substance,' retorted Lloyd Roberts. 'Education is all she lacks.'

'What does he know?' Owen's voice spilled out angrily, once out of earshot of the chapel crowd. 'The likes of him have had it easy for far too long. They've become immune to the suffering around them. Since the Amendment Act, those with nothing have to go over the mountain to Martr village to collect their measly five shillings, and it costs two shillings to get there. Don't they ever listen to what they hear on a Sunday evening? The godly look after the poor and sick. Fine for them to condemn folk for drunkenness and unseemly behaviour. What is there for the poor? Nothing but hard work for little reward. Drunkenness is a manifestation of their troubled lives.

'Oh let's get married soon, *Cariad*.' Owen grasped Angharad's limp, clammy hands. 'Let's do something. Let's make things better somehow. I see you getting to look so tired, and I see young girls getting old, girls going to the brickworks each morning. Girls who should be teachers and nurses. We could maybe set up a school.' Owen's voice gushed with enthusiasm, trying to communicate fifteen minutes worth of words within five. 'I could teach you. We could then educate others, give them hope. Things are going to change around here,' he enthused, gesturing expansively, carving the air with his hands. 'There'll be good houses, schools and hospitals. Let's bring our children up to set an example. We can show people there is a better way of living.'

'Oh, Owen,' said Angharad resignedly, turning away from him. 'I'm not clever like you. I wasn't sent to school at Tresant village. I just went to the Sunday hour school.'

'But you can read, dear Angharad, which is more than half the village can do. You are clever; you were just never given the opportunity. Why do you resent me so, Angharad?' Owens's features creased with puzzlement and hurt. 'Can't you see how happy you could be, if only you would just let me become a part of your life?' Owen's body slumped as he sought the trunk of a tree for support.

Angharad sat helplessly on a rock, eyes glazed by tears.

# Chapter 14

'She was my grandmother's sister,' Gaby's grandmother said sombrely, after handing Gaby a steaming mug of tea.

'My great grandfather Llewellyn was renting this farm at the time, and she came to work here.'

'So your great grandmother was Gwen.' A look of awareness came over Gaby.

'That's right.'

'So what happened to everyone after the case?' Gaby watched the steam rising from her mug.

'Her mother never really got over it. Well, you wouldn't, would you? Not after something like that. But she had to try, to not let it affect her other children. It wasn't really talked about. I only got to hear about it when I overheard a neighbour talking about Angharad to my Mam. I asked my Mam who Angharad was. She said it was Mamgu's sister, who died very young. When I asked questions, she just found some task to busy herself with, so I gave up after a while. I didn't find out about it until much later, when I met your Taid, and it was he who told me.'

'What happened to Owen and Gwyn?'

'Gwyn went to Australia. He was *Gwr y Gloran* down to his bones, that one, but there was nothing here for him after that. There was all talk in the village. No girl would have been interested in him; it would have been on their minds whether he actually had murdered her. Every time someone passed him, it would have been going through their minds. Well, you know what talk is like around here. The only way he could have got away from it would have been to go to Australia. They were looking for people with his skills at the time. The gold rush was happening and they were crying out for people, so he left, and that was the last anyone saw of him.

'Owen, well, he never recovered. Went to live near where she was buried—returning to the scene of the crime, some said. He visited the grave every day. He never bothered with anyone. Well, there was no talking to him, anyway; he would just babble a load of gibberish. I don't think he could cope with what happened around these parts afterwards. The coming of the pits... Well, things never did get any better. Maybe for the pit owners, who grew fat and prosperous by the irresponsible exploitation of the workers and the land, to get at the promises underneath.'

'Oh aye, the roads and the railways penetrated alright,' came the voice of Albert from his chair in the corner, 'and there was a social cost to it all. No protection from the entrepreneurs, who recklessly exploited the land and the workers. The river turned black, became a cesspit. A receptacle for all the refuse of industry and sewerage from the households.

'Large fortunes were made by those who had capital, needless to say, not for the likes of those around these parts though. Landholders ruthlessly exploited farmers, who were turfed out of their homes, as more money could be gained from the minerals under the land. Those working down the pits toiled in harsh, dangerous conditions. Excessively long hours, from six in the morning to six at night. Daylight could not reach those parts. The week became one long night. There was coal dust in the air, which got to the lungs, causing asthma and bronchitis, leading to emphysema in the long term. The owners were more concerned with output, and oblivious to the sufferings of the workers. One pit owner employed a doctor, but his salary was paid by deductions from mineworkers' pay. The march of progress.' His voice was heavy with sarcasm. 'Call that progress.'

'Wasn't all doom and gloom though,' he continued. 'Mining was a culture you see. That's all there was. Miners walked to work together, some carried their children on their shoulders. The talk in the pubs was about mining. There was a sense of community then, a sense of belonging. We were all covered by the same dust. Times were hard alright, but we stuck together.'

'All the workers and families sticking together couldn't defeat the power of the few,' came Brian's disgruntled voice. 'They were starved into submission on the strikes.'

'That was because of those blacklegs they brought in from Ireland and the North,' Gaby's grandfather said caustically. 'That's when the Union started.'

'Aye, and the pit owners formed associations of their own,' Brian retorted scornfully without looking up from his newspaper.

'It was the start,' Albert continued adamantly. 'Socialism was being spread; the new generation was educated now—there was better organisation. Even Winston himself was brought in on the Cambrian.'

'Huh, look what a mess that was,' Brian said derisively. 'Police, troops, rioting and looting.'

'There was a lot of government propaganda,' Albert's voice was louder now. 'It was to make us look bad. Only about one or two shops got looted.'

'Oh, that's alright then.'

'What do you expect? Riots start with a grievance. People had had it up to here with exploitation and corruption. There was anger; men had seen their neighbours killed in explosions. Profits had been put before safety, families torn apart. There was no compensation then.'

'There weren't cameras either, Dad. Had the jury seen photographs of the wounds, body matter exposed, there may have been a different reaction.'

'Agh, don't give me your Campbell's Act. The judges were in with the pit owners. The widows lost their houses as well as their husbands. Yes, things did get out of hand. It became a free for all. Shop owners lost their livelihoods, as had the miners over the years. Asquith was forced to bow though—the minimum wage was brought in.'

'Calm down, Albert,' Gaby's grandmother said from her knitting. 'I'll be a widow if you carry on like this. It was hard at first, but at least coal brought jobs to the area. Look at the streets today, full of youngsters on drugs. That was never the case when the pits were working.'

'Coal was a creative as well as a destructive force,' Albert's voice was calmer now. 'Look at what coal achieved. The pits were nationalised in 1947. There was a great sense of optimism. The voters had rejected Churchill and his Conservatives. What more proof do you want of the determination of people who had won a war? They were prepared to give a chance to a party that had not been in power for many years. The Labour government made people feel they had control. Manufacturing gave structure to their lives.'

'Look what happened to that dream.' Gaby's grandmother became engaged in the conversation. 'Look at all the skills going to waste, youngsters hanging about on the streets. Why aren't they becoming engineers and environmentalists, working for the good of the country? Aneurin would turn in his grave if he could see the streets today.'

'We were too reliant on one industry, that's why,' Brian argued fervently. 'We're more exposed to the wider world now. There are many industries—we need to diversify, but we are too set in our attitudes. Too isolated here. Sense of community is OK, but people need to adapt, be more flexible.'

'There's no security any longer,' Albert said insistently. 'No job for life. Thatcher changed all that, smashed manufacturing in this country. All this talk of technology. There was no technological revolution, just one hundred and fifty thousand people who lost their jobs. A new regime replaced the old and was corrupted by the same injustices.'

'You keep harping on about Thatcher, Dad. Coal is dead. There is never going to be another boom town around here. The only remains of the mining industry is that of the coal dust carried around on the miner's lungs'

'The miner may have gone,' Albert continued sulkily, 'but the culture and heritage remain. You can't take the community spirit out of the man.'

# Chapter 15

Gaby had retreated to her sanctuary by the well on the mountainside. Something had changed during these past few weeks. She could no longer see the world as she once had. She could no longer plan, so she had no idea what the next few weeks held for her, a thought that held much trepidation. The landscape was the one thing that felt unchanged, so she tried to derive comfort from it.

Maybe the essence of the land could be perceived. After all, many researchers had felt that ancient landmarks had been built in areas of mystical significance, their detection equipment uncovering areas of strong forces or powers. Was the land trying to tell her something? These broken voices of the mountains. The visible world of concrete and computers was supposed to be reality, but she often felt as if she was losing touch with this world. Her thoughts were a seal from reality. Maybe that was why she felt trapped by her private anxieties, overwhelmed by negativity. In her loneliness and isolation, she had contemplated her environment, and believed what was said to her. The news headlines were unfalteringly grim and seemed to be conveying the same message: *"Beware. The world is unsafe."*

*"What a horrible world, do I really want to be part of this? Why don't you try tranquilisers?"* someone had once suggested to her. Tranquilisers were

the anaesthetic of anxieties; she did not want to go down that route. Her world, at least, was the honest world; to try to escape that would only lead to further problems. Only she could cleanse this stain on her unhappiness; this was a problem she would need to solve.

Now however, she needed to give her mind a rest, respite from the persistent thoughts which had been taunting her for weeks now.

She had fiercely seized on the tame explanation from her grandmother.

'*Suicide*!' she had vented incredulously. 'Her head was practically severed from her body, and she was said to have done that herself! What was wrong with those people?'

'They used her pregnancy to try and provide a practical explanation,' her grandmother tried to explain. 'It was quite a stigma in those days.'

'Well, you know what the police are like,' Brian contributed his two penneth worth. 'They like a resolution. Whatever peg fitted the hole.'

A witness had testified to Angharad showing signs of moroseness. The thoughts could not leave Gaby alone. This had been interpreted as depression, depression due to her pregnancy.

Of course she would have been depressed. Had she really loved Gwyn? In that case, the man she loved, whose child she'd been carrying, had rejected her. Her romantic dreams shattered, smashed to pieces, as if by the force of his heavy iron hammer against the anvil. Had she hoped their unborn child would bond them? That they would set up an idyllic home, in a stone cottage on the side of the mountain?

What were her alternatives? A life with Owen,

a man she did not love. Would she have been able to live that lie? Could she have made that sacrifice for the sake of her child? If only she had had the benefit of an education, then she would have had options. She would have seen further than the farm, and over the mountains that enveloped her. There was more to life than marriage and children.

Gaby started speculating how things may have turned out had Angharad not been murdered. She would have probably accepted her fate and married Owen. How many children would they have had? Would they have fulfilled Owen's noble intentions, and made valid contributions to the cause of humanity? Their children may have grown up happily, even if Angharad wasn't. Their children may have gone on to have had children of their own. Gaby may have had cousins, relatives with a similar outlook to her own. She may have had someone with which to share her unconventional world. An image appeared in her mind, an image of herself in twenty years' time, taking the same train each morning. Walking into the same drab, sixties-structured building.

She often criticised those around her for their apathy at being stuck in a rut. But then, so was she. She was always grasping at something intangible. Just out of reach. Grabbing invisible air. Knowing it was there somewhere, but not knowing where. There was no guarantee that whatever was there would materialise.

Her friend Stevo was right. She needed to do something soon. It need not be groundbreaking, but if she did nothing, she would grow old with bitterness and regrets. *Angharad may not have had a choice,* she thought, *but I have. Was that what Angharad was trying to tell me?*

There had been expectations of Angharad, that she would marry Owen, a man with a future. But she chose love over money. Didn't the other villagers know what love was? Look what happened, however, when Angharad tried to defy convention. Attitudes were the trap in this place, not the mountains.

Suddenly, it became all so clear to Gaby. She would need to get away from here.

# Chapter 16

Her realisation bestowed Gaby with an optimism she had not felt for some time, feeding her with an exhilarating sense of expectation. It was as if a wet cloth had been rubbed across a dirt-encrusted window pane. She was swept back to the weeks leading up to Christmas when she was a child. Christmas was one of the cherished memories in the storage room of her mind. She was captivated by the anticipation from the glitter and colourful lights adorning every house and shop.

This renewed state of mind launched her into a course of action and determination. She was hardly able to sleep that night and restlessly awaited the morning, when she could fulfil her resolution and turn her thoughts into reality, instead of her reality being her thoughts.

She hastened to the library after a hurried breakfast.

'Had a groundbreaking idea on that murder case, have you?' the librarian greeted her jovially.

'Do you have any journals advertising job vacancies?'

'Looking for a change from the detective profession, are we? Best place to start would be the jobs sections in the newspapers. If you're still interested in that murder case though, that article you asked me to look for was written by a local man. A retired history teacher.'

'Oh great! Have you got the article?'

'Yes, but why bother with the article when you can speak to him face to face? I'm sure he wouldn't be difficult to find—just contact the school.'

'Yeah, that's a good idea, thanks.'

Gaby keenly proceeded to the newspaper holders, where she spread a national newspaper over the large table. After two tall pages of requests for medical specialists or political strategists, bold lettering struck her with the impact of being hit by the arrows of twenty archers.

*EMIGRATE TO AUSTRALIA. DO IT TODAY*

She squandered no time in taking down the details, which charged her with a new sense of purpose. A new beginning illuminated before her, her choices suddenly became three dimensional. She made an appointment with the recruiting agent and began an agonising eight day wait.

The man at the recruiting agency had inspired her further.

'There are always employers looking for someone with experience in accounts,' he had said. 'They could always use someone with enthusiasm, and you would have no problem adapting to the different accounting regulations that apply to the country.'

Not all those closest to her shared her elation, however.

'This will be such a great opportunity,' she pleaded to her mother.

'But do you have to go to the other end of the earth?'

'There's nothing for me around here. What are we? A road going through the mountains, with houses either side.'

'Don't worry, June, she'll be back in six months,' her father had said wryly.

'Some peace and quiet at last,' said Jonathan. 'I'll have the bathroom to myself on Friday nights.'

Her grandmother was grim and tight lipped. 'What on earth is there in Australia that you can't get here?'

'Sun, for one thing,' Brian piped up.

'Many of our ancestors left for a better life in Australia,' said Gaby.

'They felt they had no option,' said her grandmother. 'The coal industry was in decline, the depression hit the area hard. Conditions in the mines were not improving, with wages being cut and hours increased. Many colliers were starved back to work in the general strike. You don't realise how lucky you are, my girl. You have a good job, a decent young man. Many a lady would like to be in your position.'

'I don't want to be filling in forms for the rest my life in some dead-end office,' Gaby protested. 'I've had enough of the highlight of my week being the Emerald Tree every Friday night. I want to experience so much more,' she implored. 'There is a world out there, something beyond these mountains. I don't want to spend my life cooking and changing nappies.'

'What's wrong with marriage and children?' her grandmother retorted indignantly. 'It did me alright.'

'May have been alright for you, but it's not for me.'

'This is what you get when you give women an education.' Brian grinned.

'Things were different in my day,' said her grandmother, slowly shaking her head.

'They certainly were,' said Brian, still grinning.

*  *  *

'Hang on a minute,' said Mickey later, at the side of the mountain where they had agreed to meet. 'I mean, this is a bit sudden, I don't know if I want to move that far.'

'Oh, but we won't be going together,' said Gaby with a look of astonishment.

'You're breaking up with me?' Mickey looked crestfallen

'Oh, Mickey, surely you didn't think this was going to last forever.'

'I don't understand, we get along so well, everything is great between us. I can tell you things I can't tell anyone else, not even Bobbit, and you want to throw all that away?' Mickey said, baffled, and Gaby noticed the pain in his voice.

'It's not throwing it all away. The last two years have been wonderful, but you've known all along that I don't intend on tying myself down.'

'Not with me at least,' Mickey said angrily. 'I'm not good enough for you, I suppose. Just because I work all day on a machine.'

'Oh, Mickey, it's nothing to do with that. I couldn't care less what you do. I just need to move on; it wouldn't matter who I was with.'

'Why go to the other side of the earth though? Couldn't you have thought of somewhere a bit further, Jupiter maybe?'

'This is a great opportunity for me, to start a new life.'

'It will be that alright, no chance of the trappings of your current life getting in the way,' Mickey said bitterly.

# Chapter 17

Gaby made her way to Mayberry Street where Mr Edmunds, the retired history teacher, lived. She had traced him through one of Brian's friends.

*'Historic Eddy,'* his friend had said, *'Ever such a nice bloke. I bumped into him a few times after I left school. He was always pleased to talk about Bryn Sec, and what a pity it had to come to an end. I don't think he could handle it when he went to the Comp. My brother used to tell me the kids played him up something rotten. Sad really, he was such a nice guy.'*

Mr Edmunds had given her directions over the telephone when he had agreed to see her. Mayberry Street was in the same part of the village as the library and was known as the more prosperous area of the community. Indeed, the streets became lined with trees as she got nearer to the area noted on the paper in her hand.

The streets consisted of large, Victorian, terraced houses. The front gardens were small with low walls, some benefiting from iron railings. There were posts either side of the metal gates, which were topped with some sort of stone ornamentation, a quadrilateral pyramid or a kind of sculpture.

Gaby arrived at number nineteen, the home of Mr Edmunds. There was a deep porch before the solid, wooden door, which was painted a glossy, deep green. Gaby admired the richly patterned porcelain tiles on the walls of the porch.

She stood there awhile, nervously smoothing her hair, before tentatively tapping the heavy brass door-knocker. She waited awkwardly for a few minutes, before hearing a shuffling from behind the door.

An elderly gentleman carefully opened the door. Gaby recognised him as one of the men who sat socialising on the park bench from time to time; some sucked on pipes. They would acknowledge passing pedestrians if not engrossed in discussion. He was around five feet nine inches tall, immaculately dressed in trousers of thick material and a tweed jacket. His shirt was of a chequered wool blend, and a paisley cravat sprouted between the opened buttons at the neck. His cheeks, which may once have been rosy, were now sallow. His hair was a dull grey yet immaculately groomed and thick despite his advanced years. In fact, the passage of time had not seemed to have affected him adversely, as it had with other men of his age.

'You must be Gaby.' He had a kind voice and refined smile, which showed just a little of his teeth.

'Yes,' Gaby replied. 'Thank you ever so much for agreeing to see me.'

'I'm most pleased you came. I'm George Edmunds, by the way.' He opened the door wider, turned to the side and beckoned her into his home.

She lingered in the hallway, before a long passageway that ended in a dim room.

'Please, go inside.' He extended his arm, open palmed, towards a room on her left.

The sitting room was medium sized, untidy and

cluttered, and smelt like her elderly aunt's house. Books and papers were scattered over the floor and table in a chaos of academia. Bookshelves were stuffed to overflowing, papers spilled onto the window ledge. One wall was entirely lined by bookshelves.

'Would you like to sit here?' Mr Edmunds said, removing a stack of magazines from an armchair. 'You'll be able to see the cherry blossom from this chair.'

The chair faced a window that overlooked a small square garden, bordered by a clutter of variegated flowers and bushes. Petals and leaves were strewn across the grass square, in the middle of which stood a proud tree with a head of pink hair.

'Please ignore the mess,' he continued good-naturedly. 'I'm afraid the place has got quite out of hand, since my dear wife, Dorothy, passed away. It would have been six years ago now.'

'I'm sorry,' Gaby said awkwardly.

'Don't worry, my dear. We all have to go some time. But you are far too young to be even contemplating death. Can I get you a cup of tea, or a glass of port?' he enquired.

He was mild mannered and courteous, and Gaby started to feel at ease.

'No, I'm fine, thanks.'

'Would you mind if I had a glass?' He opened the glass doors of a cabinet and moved a box of packet soups from the shelf before taking out a bottle of port, with which he half filled a thick, crystal glass. 'It is encouraging to see a young mind so interested in the past. I wish more people would study history. The role of the historian is to remember what others forget. Kids today, however'—he raised his glass to the light provided by the window, scrutinising the rich ruby liquid inside, like a connoisseur examining a rarer brand of port—'they are not interested in the past. This is the technological generation, of games machines and action films. Teachers of other subjects regard history as an irrelevance, inferior to their subjects,' he said with a slight distaste.

He sat back in an armchair. 'We all have a history. Even one as young as you, albeit a short one.' He smiled a decorous smile.

Gaby noticed some photographs on the wall. One of a young man and woman, and two black and white photographs of a wedding couple, the man dressed in a naval uniform.

'Do you have children?' she enquired.

'Yes, a boy and a girl'.

'Are they interested in history?'

'The boy is an archaeologist, and my daughter a photographer. So yes, photography is history, in a way, I suppose. Photographs are snapshots of the past. We are after all, products of our past.'

Gaby returned his amiable smile.

'So you're interested in the Ty Coch murder.' He held the sentence ponderously, as if weighing it. 'Very tragic business,' he said, shaking his head slightly. 'Very tragic. Such a young life, a couple with a future ahead of them.'

'Terrible', Gaby agreed. 'From beginning to end.'

'Did it really end?' Mr Edmunds raised his eyebrows slightly. 'After all, you are still questioning the event, despite the passing of over a hundred years.'

'The power of history.' Gaby smiled.

'Indeed,' he agreed, with a glint to his eye. 'So tell me, my dear, how can I help you?'

Gaby recounted the facts she had compiled as a result of her research, and leapt into her questions.

'Why did Owen rush out so soon after the service? Wouldn't it have made more sense to check whether Llewellyn, or anyone else in the congregation, had seen Angharad, and why take the long route back to the farm? If he was so keen to find her, the short route would have been quicker.'

'We don't always act rationally when in a panic,' Mr Edmunds said warmly. 'Maybe it was as he had said, and he took the long route back because he had already taken the short route, so he knew he had not seen Angharad there. Had he taken the short route, he would have touched Angharad, so would invariably have had blood on his clothes. Maybe God was with him that night, as some would say.'

'What happened to Owen after he had left the farm on finding Angharad was not there? He said he was going to search for her. How come he did not come across the body if his search was so thorough? Why use a razor to commit the act? Surely it would have been a lot easier to have used a sickle, which Gwyn would have had access to. It would also have been easier for Owen to get the sickle from the barn, as opposed to entering the house to get Gwyn's razor.'

'He would have looked pretty conspicuous walking around with a sickle. A razor would have been much easier to hide. There was the case of Constance Kent just prior to the Ty Coch murder—

she killed her baby brother with a razor. Would have got away with it had she not confessed years later. No one would believe that a lady of such well breeding would have been capable of such an act. Owen would probably have been held in the same regard,' Mr Edmunds said politely.

'What do you think about Gwyn?' Gaby asked. 'And the fact that he went straight to bed without enquiring about Angharad?'

'Well, it could certainly be argued that Gwyn had a motive. Angharad's demands on him were becoming oppressive. His hopes that she would marry her betrothed and be removed from his life were quickly fading, placing him in an unwelcome dilemma. She wasn't getting the message, despite his lack of encouragement. She may even have been using the threat of the unborn child against him. Her aunt and uncle would not have liked that. They would have given him an ultimatum, either face up to his responsibilities or find a job elsewhere. His friends and family would put pressure on him to marry her. He wouldn't have got alternative work around these parts; he would be ostracised from the community. Doesn't mean to say he killed her, however, but she did seem to be becoming an irritant in his life. Maybe he was glad she was not at the farm on his return, and went straight to bed to avoid her. Not wanting to ask after her, he didn't want to encourage any supposition.'

'His razor was at the scene of the crime with no blood on it.' Gaby continued hypothesising. 'Surely he wouldn't leave such obvious evidence behind if he was the murderer? What about the fact that it was planted there to make it look like suicide?

If Gwyn had done so, he would either have used another more efficient weapon and placed the razor there, in which case, why didn't he brush the razor in the blood? The wound indicated the victim was left handed. For those who believed the ridiculous theory that the act was committed by the victim, Gwendolyn and Owen testified to not being aware of this. If Owen was the guilty one, surely it would have been to his benefit to say she was left handed and ensure the razor had blood on it. Gwyn had not noticed, yet the stable boy, Taliesin, confirmed she was. Taliesin seemed to be testifying much in Gwyn's favour. I wonder if Gwyn had any influence over him?'

'Interesting.' Mr Edmund's eyes narrowed thoughtfully. 'This was not the act of a cold-blooded killer. Once accomplished, the perpetrator may have been overcome with such a horror as to be rendered incapable of any further deed, and just fled the scene.'

'But they both could be accounted for at the time of death,' Gaby persisted.

'How reliable were forensics in those days?' Mr Edmunds replied calmly. 'There was not the technical accuracy of today. I would not, therefore, put such faith in the time of death.'

'But *suicide*,' Gaby said with consternation. 'Surely people realised the impossibility of the situation.'

'You have to understand the times they were living in. It was a very close-knit community. People did not want to believe that such a horrendous act could take place in a village that took pride in its piety and humanity. There was also the reputation of the village to consider.'

'If they did not want to believe that of their fellow man, didn't they consider that it may have been a serial killer who was not a resident of the village?'

'A stranger just passing through.' Mr Edmunds pursed his lips quizzically. 'In a village where everyone knew each other? Such an itinerant would not have gone unnoticed. Besides, there would have been other such murders, and there were no others recorded. Death by suicide was a much more convenient verdict. The victim had, after all, been morose and tearful. The stigma of pregnancy outside marriage was viewed as a strong enough motive. Had there been photographs of the wounds inflicted, I daresay the jury would have reached a different conclusion. The decision also eliminated any fear in the community that there was a murderer on the loose.'

'So justice went by the wayside, and they just buried their heads in the sand,' Gaby said disparagingly.

'The disadvantages outweighed righteousness. Bear in mind there was very little precedent. The detective as a professional had not been established that long. JPs held sway, assisted by a petty constable to maintain law and order. Such miscarriages do still occur today,' Mr Edmunds said with a slight air of authority, 'only today we have the appeals process, so it is not so easy to escape retribution. There was also talk about the uncle.'

'*Llew,*' Gaby exclaimed incredulously.

'Well, you know what gossip is like around here,' Mr Edmunds said with a twinkle of amusement in his eyes. 'That the baby may have been his and she was about to expose the fact. Imagine the shame and humiliation, not only on the uncle but on his family.'

'I can't believe the depths people will sink to, to say such a thing.' Gaby's voice was heavy with contempt.

'Such things have only become apparent in the past twenty years. Apparently it happened in some rural communities. I don't think so much in the South Wales communities though.'

Gaby's head was shaking in disbelief.

'Are you sure you won't take any refreshment?' Mr Edmunds said benignly. 'I'm very much aware we've been talking for well over an hour and you haven't taken a drink.'

'No, I'm fine honestly. Do you like living here?'

'I've lived here a long time and seen many changes. We're still a nice community, although it is not as good as it was in the old days.'

'Was that when all the mines were working?'

'Oh yes,' Mr Edmunds said emphatically. 'We were a coal metropolis then. Coal was God, but miners were the sacrificial lambs. Food was put on the table by coal, which was extracted by starvation and poverty. Things got better though, over time.' Mr Edmunds' gaze seemed to be fixed on a spot on the wall in front of him.

'Was your father a miner?'

'No, no. My father was a draftsman. He drew plans for the mines. All that is gone now,' he said with a hint of melancholy in his voice. 'Nothing ever replaced the coal industry. Factories were built as there was a supply of labour, particularly female labour, which was cheaper then. But it was never the same. Now, even that's all gone.'

'How about your job, did you enjoy teaching?'

'I did, until the comprehensive system was brought in. Grammar schools were much better—they had character. Comprehensives were all about cramming as many children as possible into a school.'

'I guess the population was large.'

'Nonsense. Families were large in my day; my mother had four of us, and that was considered small.'

'I guess those children grew up to have children of their own, in which case the population would have quadrupled.'

'Fair point,' he conceded. 'I did find myself at a loss when I retired, however, which was why I took up studying local history.' His eyes went to the clock on the mantelpiece. 'Good gracious, is that the time? It's been almost two hours that we've been talking.'

'Well, I won't keep you any longer.' Gaby stood up. 'Thank you ever so much for speaking with me today. You have cleared matters up for me no end.'

'Not at all, it was a pleasure, my dear. It isn't every day one has the opportunity of discussing past events with such a delightful young mind.'

Mr Edmunds accompanied Gaby to the door, where they shook hands before parting. On reaching the end of the street, Gaby turned back to see Mr Edmunds still standing outside the porch. He gave her a final wave before she disappeared around the corner.

# Chapter 18

Gaby awoke that morning from another twisted, tangled sleep. She had dreamt again of Angharad, and felt the heaviness of the day ahead weighing densely on her mind, until she realised she had woken to a Sunday. A day of reliable tedium. She lay there contemplating how she was going to manage the unusable hours that dragged out before her like a blank sheet of paper, as if in a geography examination for which she had not sufficiently prepared.

She took in the familiar pattern of the wallpaper and how, on a Sunday, everything appeared different. Languid and inert, in league with the Almighty on this day of rest. Such mellowness was not in synchrony with Gaby's nature however, and she would need to expend much effort in applying herself to a day where motion seemed to have slowed down, like the distorted sounds from a radio whose batteries were coming towards their end.

Her Sunday morning chore was to take out the rubbish. She remained outside for a while, idly watching a large beetle scurrying along the path. She wondered about its purpose in life. What an uncomplicated life, just to remain alive.

The rest of the morning would be spent passively, trifling with activities such as reading the newspaper and lounging in front of the television, watching un-engaging programmes. Then there was the family tradition of taking lunch with her grandparents. Maybe she would go for a swim mid-afternoon to break up the day a little, and then there was the church service in the early evening. Sometimes she met Mickey in the afternoons after a swim at the local leisure centre, but she didn't want to spend the time appeasing and appealing to him. Communication between them had been difficult since she had announced her intentions regarding Australia. They had walked wordlessly, side by side, down from the mountain. He had accused her of being heartless. She hadn't meant to be callous; after all, she had never misled him about her intentions.

*'You're living in a dream world,'* he had railed against her. *'I don't know what's come over you these past few weeks, since this ghost came into your life. It's not real, can't you see that?'*

There was an ocean of misunderstanding between them. This was not her world; she felt a foreigner here. She had no desire to paddle at the shallow end of the ocean. She had decided to swim. The love she felt for him was an artificial love. A love she wanted to feel, the kind she read about in books, or saw in films.

She did not get to go swimming in the afternoon. The conversation amongst the Sunday aroma of roast meat and cabbage was directed at her, regarding her pending move to Australia.

'I don't know what she hopes to achieve by going to the other end of the earth,' said her mother with disdain. 'She has everything she needs here—a good job, a nice boy.'

'You've indulged her too much,' her grandmother added. 'We made do with what we had in my day, and we didn't have half of what these youngsters have. They get things too easy—that's the problem—and they just want more and more.'

'Big ideas, that's what she's got,' said Jonathan teasingly.

'I don't exactly see you contributing much around here,' Gaby snapped with annoyance. She turned angrily to her mother and grandmother. 'You never moan at him, do you? He can lounge about the place, sit in front of the television for hours on end, be waited on hand and foot, and you never so much as raise an eyebrow at him.'

'Bring back National Service I say,' Albert threw in, from his armchair near the television. 'Then they'd have a shock.'

'The war effort doesn't mean anything anymore.' Gaby rounded on Albert. 'People aren't interested in that today. You go on about the sacrifices made so we could have a better life, but it is no better. Nobody gives a damn that there are no jobs in the villages. The villages are being left to rot. People are living practically hand to mouth on the estate. Injustice went on before the war, and it's going on now. A woman can be found with her head separated from her body, and six men said she had done it herself! What kind of justice is that?' Gaby stormed out of the house.

She headed over the mountain with vigour, her mind in a rage. *If they think I've had it so easy,* she ruminated, *they want to try living my life.*

She crossed fields where battles had once taken place, sharing the space of those Bronze Age warriors. A monolithic stone defiantly stood in the field, a piece of the past surviving in the present. There were many such megalithic landmarks dotted around the villages. Impressive revelations of nature, exalting, menacing, the land trying to tell its secret life. Gaby paused to catch her breath.

There was stillness here, the stillness of an eternal beginning. The world as it had always been, a state of non-being. Gaby looked at her watch. *That can't be*. She must have been there at least half an hour, yet her watch had not recorded that. It still showed the time as four o'clock.

She felt an involuntary shudder, which impelled her to move onwards. Realising that her watch had stopped and she had no idea of the time, she decided to make her way to church. She would not have time to go back and change out of her jeans.

She walked briskly up the path, the only sound being that of her trainers scrunching on the loose, small stones from the gravel crumbling beneath her thick soles. *This is the path that Angharad would have taken, over a hundred years ago*, the thoughts started up again. She wondered what Angharad would have been feeling that night. Was she full of anticipation—as was Gaby, due to her relocation to another country—or foreboding? Was she going to tell Owen that she would not marry him, hoping he would not get upset and beg her, otherwise she would be forced to tell him she was pregnant by another man? Was she still clinging to the dream of marrying Gwyn? He was not clever like Owen, who was seen as the more successful suitor, but love was not a matter of choice.

The words of the pastor at last Sunday's

service thrust into Gaby's thoughts, *'The truth shall set you free.'* How she would love to be free. Unencumbered by anxiety and apprehension. The image of Saul on the road to Damascus entered her mind. Her science teacher had believed Saul to have been under the influence of mescaline when he experienced his conversion. Mescaline, he'd said, was grown in the area.

The brightness of the sun took on a metallic glare. The light around her became more intense and white. The trees and plants around her burned in a verdant blaze. The land around her seemed to be breathing. The ground throbbed and trembled beneath her. The mountain felt as if it was shuddering. She heard a creaking from below the ground and vaguely registered the faint sound of bells declaring a Sunday, which seemed discordant with the surrounding sounds. She thought she heard her name being shouted. Was she hearing the voice of the mountain?

The violence of the landscape kept her from dwelling on this. The slope felt as if it was getting steeper and steeper, although her senses told her this could not be so. Thorns from nearby bushes clung to her clothing, pulling her back. The stones underfoot appeared to be jumping up at her. She felt as if the force of the mountain was being unleashed upon her, oppressive yet magnetic.

Her mind was speeding out of control; she wiped her forehead with the back of her hand, and was surprised to feel glistening perspiration. Her world constricted and her vision was narrowing. She slowly slipped into that state between dream and daylight, where everything merges and mingles. She lifted her billowing skirt to carry her faster, exposing her brown, laced-up boots, which were scraping against the small, loose stones beneath them. She felt the tiny kick inside her and became filled with the vision of new life. A new life with the farm boy.

He was not receptive to her plans at the moment. Things would change however. Once she had broken with Owen, once he would come around to accepting life as a husband and father. He had reservations, of course. He had never needed to take care of anyone before. He was living a meaningless life, smashing up wood every day and ploughing the fields, or down the Seren of an evening, trying to make the monotony more bearable. The new life she carried inside her would give them purpose.

She had made up her mind to tell Owen this evening, and she felt sick with apprehension at the approaching moment. She would have to tell him about Gwyn, as he was just not accepting the fact that she did not want to marry him, even though she had twice turned down his entreaties.

He was there in the usual place where she met him every Sunday evening before Chapel, leaning against a tree. Trepidation rose in her. His undaunted smile, forewarning that this was not going to be an easy task. He straightened up on seeing her approach. His smile quickly disappeared, however, and his face became anxious as she got closer to him.

'What is wrong, my love?' he said with concern, taking both her hands in his. 'You look pale and weary.'

Angharad smiled weakly.

'Oh, what have I done to you?' Owen took

her into his arms and pulled her unyielding body close to him. 'I've been putting too much pressure on you lately. Trying to rush you into something, when you need more time to be convinced. How selfish I have been. It's just that I've found the woman with whom I want to spend the rest of my life, and I want that life to start as soon as possible.'

Angharad sagged under the weight of knowing the enormity of what she had to say.

'Oh, Owen.' She gently turned away from him and summoned all the strength she had within her in order to tell him what she had made up her mind to. 'Why can't you understand?' Tears softly burned her eyes; she did not dare to look at his face. 'It's not you I want. I can't see you again. I'm pregnant, and you know it's not by you.'

Owen staggered back in mortification. The look of disbelief in his eyes slowly faded into a smile of cold derision. He stared at her for a few moments in stunned silence. He turned from her without saying a word and retreated back down the bridle track.

Angharad tried to compose herself, and continued blunderingly up the track, full of reproach over what she had just done. Kind, gentle Owen, who had never done anything bad in his life. How she had hurt him. He didn't deserve this. If only he had not met her, he could have found someone more worthy of his love. Someone good and reliable, who would have made him a good wife. They would have had children together, and would have been so happy.

Angharad was startled out of her thoughts by the sharp sound of twigs being stepped on and snapped. She swung around and was overcome with surprise.

'*You,*' she exclaimed with shock, in a voice that was not hers.

# Chapter 19

Gaby had the sensation of floating on a raft, being softly rocked by gentle waters. Her drifting bliss was abruptly cut short by the chemical smell which assaulted her nostrils, a sharpness that scratched at the back of her throat. Her eyes opened to a stark, white, sterile brightness, which caused her to immediately clench her eyelids tightly back together again.

Little by little, her eyelids parted until her retina had adjusted to the artificial glare. The ceiling was unrecognisable, so she turned to the walls, which were also unfamiliar. She tried to sit up, but found the effort too arduous. She struggled to recall the previous evening, desperately trying to find something that made sense, but her mind was so bruised and battered that even the process of thinking made her feel tired.

'Woken up, have we?' The chirpy voice belonged to a woman in her thirties, of average height and build, who was wearing a starched, white uniform. Her hair was a mid-brown, but Gaby was unable to deduce anything further, as it was bundled into a small, white cap.

'Where am I?' Gaby's voice felt thick and heavy.

'You're in hospital, love,' returned the blithe, cheerful voice.

'How did I get here?' The attempt to speak required much exertion. It was as if her tongue was swollen to three times its normal size.

'You were brought in last night. You were found unconscious on the side of Brynhalig.'

'My grandmother will be so worried.' Gaby almost sprang upright, but was hit by a wave of dizziness, like the slamming of brakes on a car, which caused her to fall back onto the yielding firmness of the hospital bed.

'Lie back down, and don't worry. Your family know where you are. They were all here last night, and your boyfriend. The doctor sent them home eventually. He told them you were suffering from exhaustion and just needed total rest. There was nothing they could do, apart from getting some rest themselves. Now, I'll leave you to relax. Breakfast will be along in ten minutes— make sure you eat well, you'll need to get your strength up.'

Gaby lay back against the pillow, and felt a peace she had not experienced for some time, and not just from the quiet and cleanliness of the hospital, but a feeling of relief. A sense that something had been accomplished, some sort of resolution. She was certain that Owen had committed the murder. *So it was Owen then,* Gaby thought with a soothing satisfaction. He had gone storming off down the path, thoughts of Angharad, Gwyn and the unborn child ruminating in his mind. Mulling the thoughts until they took possession of him. He could stand it no longer; he would put an end to it. A rage so intense that it drove him to repeatedly slash at her throat with such ferocity, a fury that overcame all compassion and rationality. Owen, so gentle and considerate, must have been driven to distraction to commit an act of such savagery.

'You gave us quite a fright.' Mickey appeared in the doorway, where he stood with his fists in the pockets of his tight black jeans, his face contorted by restrained distress, whilst Gaby was eating cereal and toast. 'We were shouting all over the mountain, looking for you, and it was pitch black. Thank goodness for torches and a full moon is all I can say.'

'What time were you shouting?' Gaby enquired.

'Oh, it must have been from ten o'clock onwards, why?

'I remember someone shouting my name, but it was only about an hour after I had left.'

'It couldn't have been. I didn't get the call from your Mam until about nine. She wanted to know if you were with me. I said I hadn't seen you all day. She then went on about some things she had said, and she wished she hadn't said them. Well, after that, we were frantically ringing around everybody.'

'Hey, Gabs, glad to see you back in the land of the living. You had us all worried there for a while.' Jonathan breezed into the room.

'That must have been a first, worried about me. I bet, really, you were thinking, great, bathroom to myself, no moaning when rugby has been on the telly for about ten hours.'

'Hmmm, come to think of it... Mam and Nan are really sorry about the things they said yesterday; they feel so guilty.'

'Nothing to do with them, I'm fine now. I just want to come home.'

'Missing rugby on the telly, are you? You've got to have a few tests before they let you out.'

'You'll have the house to yourself a bit longer then.' Gaby sighed and laid her head back against the pillow.

# Chapter 20

Gaby sank into the plush upholstery of the backseat of the taxi as the door snapped shut with the sound of finality. Rubber against rubber, sealing her into safety. She relished the excitement of her impending adventure churning within her as the taxi rolled along the quiet stretch of road from her grandmother's house. The house and fields slowly shrank in the rear-view mirror. She gazed down at the length of the village unravelling before her, every crevice and undulation as familiar to her as the faces of family and friends.

She would have liked to have framed this scene, and taken it with her. She pondered over whether she had any misgivings about leaving her home town. No, she was ready; she'd had an optimistic sense of hope since the morning of the hospitalisation. It was as if she could see with a new mode of vision. Once the option of Australia had presented itself to her, she had spent the next few weeks putting in place the necessary arrangements for her departure. She wished she had known of this possibility earlier, as she could have used this plan to sustain her over times of despondency. She now awoke each morning with a sense of purpose. Her family had been keen for her to get as much rest as possible after her return from hospital, but she had felt rejuvenated. No amount of reassurance from her could dispel their fears, however, despite the fact that the tests had found no abnormalities. The only explanation the doctor could give was that it was one of those phenomena that cannot be accounted for.

She had broached the subject of Angharad. He had not been receptive, however. *'I believe there are some things that science cannot explain,'* he had said. *'But the more likely explanation is that you may have lost your grip on reality, which can sometimes happen when people have been under considerable pressure.'*

She still thought about the murder, but it no longer troubled her. She was convinced that Owen had murdered Angharad. Her mission being thus accomplished, there was no necessity for her to continue with her research, much to the relief of those close to her, especially Mickey.

'You've been spending too much time wrapped up in that murder case,' her mother had admonished. 'It's no wonder you went funny. That's enough to drive anyone mad. Why can't you spend your time studying something useful or helping me around the house?'

'Yeah, why don't you study the roulette wheel?' chipped in Jonathan cheerfully.

'I don't see you doing anything of much use,' Gaby retorted. 'Drinking, playing rugby, and when you're not playing it, you're watching it on the telly.'

'Nothing wrong with the wonderful game; it didn't send me collapsing on the side of a mountain.'

'Get out,' Gaby said and threw a cushion at him, which he caught in mid-air.

'Now I'll go for the try,' he said playfully, running into the middle of the room, where he bent to place the cushion on the floor with one hand.

She looked back to that last afternoon she had spent with Mickey a little way up the mountain. Just behind Mountain View, where they sat in the warm, afternoon sunshine on a small wall, overlooking the last row of houses. The wall might have been used to enclose a farmer's field at some point in time. Lichen had formed an aged skin over the uneven large stones, supplied by local geology. Part of the wall had collapsed due to neglect, the remains clinging to the mountain like a decaying molar.

That last afternoon had gone better than she had anticipated. Mickey had accepted that she was leaving, and had been mercifully upbeat about the subject.

'He must have loved her very much,' Gaby said intriguingly.

'You're not still going on about that murder case are you? Give it a rest, or your Mam will be killing *you*,' he said, looking at her with raised eyebrows and widened eyes.

'To be driven to do such a thing must have taken a love so strong.'

'How could it have been? You don't kill someone you love,' Mickey said derisively.

'He couldn't bear to be without her.'

'Bit stupid killing her then, init? Then he really was without her.'

'He couldn't cope with the thought that he could lose her love.'

'He'd already lost it. That was something you do on impulse. He just lost control; it was spur of the moment.'

'It wasn't though. He didn't do it straight away. He left her, and about twenty minutes had passed before he returned to seek her out. He had twenty minutes to think about it. How Gwyn had crushed his dreams, like a cuckoo ruthlessly smashing the eggs of another's nest. The rage burning up inside him, each destructive thought adding fuel to the flames, until he was consumed by the fire '

'You don't know this. Just because you had some kind of illusion before you passed out.'

'It wasn't an illusion that just happened,' she had protested. 'I know the difference between dream and reality. I actually saw Owen. This was something more. Something had been leading me in this direction for weeks, maybe years. He left Angharad, went back to the house,' she continued, each word deliberate, 'and he either stole into the house and took Gwyn's razor, or maybe he took the razor when he had called at the house to enquire about her. Maybe…'

'Maybe she was murdered by a vampire,' said Mickey impatiently. 'Oh, I can't believe we're talking about this again. Talking about killing,' he said with a glint of amusement, 'did you know, there are more things in Australia that can kill you than anywhere else in the world? Australia has the ten most poisonous snakes in the world; it has the box jellyfish, sharks, the funnel-web spider to name just a few, and do *not* pick up any fluffy looking caterpillars.'

'Ugh, I hate spiders.' Gaby shuddered.

'What are you doing going to Australia, then?'

'Stop talking about such scary things. My Mam and Nan are freaking me out as it is. Worrying about me collapsing and being baked black by the sun. The only person being positive is Jonathan, and that's only because he has somewhere to stay when the All Blacks play. Let's talk about nice things, like kangaroos and Ayers Rock—what a spectacular monolith! Australia also has buried within its geological layers some of the oldest things found on earth.'

'What, even older than Miners' Row!' Mickey said with mock astonishment.

Gaby became pensive again. 'I wonder how Owen felt on realising his plan hadn't worked? He wanted to place the blame on Gwyn. Gwyn would pay for ruining his life. Yet Gwyn walked away, scot free.'

'Then he went to Aussie land, never to be seen again. Maybe bitten by the dreaded funnel spider,' said Mickey, holding his palm above her head, wriggling his spread-eagled fingers.

'Oh, there's no talking to you. Come on, let's go to the dairy; I'll buy you an ice cream.'

She did bump into him a few days later, whilst shopping near the library. He had been to sign up for a mechanics course.

'Why, that's great, Mickey!' she had enthused. 'I always thought you were wasted at that factory.'

'Well, I've always been interested in cars,' he said matter-of-factly.

'Good for you; I wish you all the best.'

'Yeah, you too. Best of luck in the land down under.'

All the time they had been together, she had tried to persuade him to do something with his life. It had taken their split for him to actually do something.

'Maybe he thought he could win you back,' Maria had suggested. 'He was awfully down the first week after your breakup.'

Gaby was glad, whatever the reason; he had something to focus on. She'd been concerned he might have fallen into despair when she left. He had finally seen sense. He did not have to stagnate, even if the area around him did.

Well, it had come around at last. Gaby once again focussed on the passing scenery from the taxi's backseat. She started to drift back into dreamland. Both Owen and Gwyn had been acquitted by a jury, but had either of them escaped payment? Owen certainly had not; he never got over Angharad's death. Was he tortured by guilt for the remainder of his life?

Gaby was instantly jolted from her reverie by the slamming of the car breaks. She lurched towards the windscreen, just catching a glimpse of a figure running in front of the car.

'Bloody Hell!' said the driver. 'Where the devil did she come from, and where has she *gone*?' He was pale faced, his jaw agape. 'She just seemed to disappear into thin air,' he said incredulously. 'Are you OK, love?'

'Yeah, I'm OK, just a bit startled.'

'Well, at least it shows my brakes are in order,' he said with an attempt at humour before continuing with the drive.

Gaby turned to look out the back window, to see a figure standing in the middle of the field. It was Angharad. She waved leisurely, and Gaby turned her whole body so she would be able to see Angharad for as long as possible. Angharad turned and seemed to be half skipping across the field, with Gaby's eyes fixed on her back.

Gaby turned back to face forward and settled comfortably into her seat to enjoy the rest of the ride. She had a pleasant feeling of liberation. Something had ended, closed, so she could move on to the next stage of her life.

# Epilogue

Warmth, brightness and a riot of colour flooded through the opened door, as if the barrier gates of a dam had been released. Gaby stepped out into the sunlight and suburbia of a Saturday morning. She proceeded down the long path to the end of the manicured lawn. Gardens here could become Miltonian paradises, crammed full of exotic plants, gorging on the nutrients supplied by a fat, round sun. She was surprised by the lush vegetation she would see growing in gardens and parks. Such foliage was unexpected in a land where the sun beat the earth every day with a constant pressure of heat. She applied sun cream liberally each day, as her skin would fry if she was not careful.

She turned right onto the sidewalk so she could take the long route to the sea. This route would take her through the cafes and pretty neon commerce. She would walk beside the continually moving cars, taking in the vibrancy and music of the city, listening to the sunshine. She had absorbed city life. Her body had adjusted to the heat like a thermostat. The airport doors had opened before her without needing to be pushed; it was as if they had known she was arriving. A new era had begun.

People had warned her that cities could be lonely, unfriendly places, but how could she be lonely? The city was alive. A living, breathing entity, even the empty spaces were inhabited, and there were plenty of empty spaces. There were areas so vast they had no shape. Even the sky appeared much larger, high and expansive, a never-ending plain of azure blue. She had no need of people, even though there were plenty around.

The Australians she had got to know were easy-going and comfortable with strangers. They had a relaxed manner, lacking in reserve, and this was very palatable. The place was magical, and she relished the freedom and novelty in her new-found life. Having found the place for which she had been searching, she no longer felt the restless impulses which had plagued her previously. She felt like a pupil who had suddenly graduated from a grim, public school. It was as if the world had been washed, and made sweeter somehow. Maybe honey had been added to the washing water.

The emancipation was delicious; she awoke every morning to a golden world of exotic and unfamiliar sounds, beckoning a day full of promise and possibility. Summers here were loud, colourful and never ending. Ripples of heat evaporated from the shimmering tarmac of the wide road, which separated the expansive, one-storey houses. Sun spilled relentlessly from a cloudless sky over low rooftops onto steaming, well-trimmed lawns.

She loved these breezeless mornings, as she glided along, singing a simply tuned song to herself. *'I hear those sounds from the city, which are sounds so pretty.'*

She seemed to belong to the sidewalks and

traffic. She had an appetite for this life; she owned the hot, blue day. She reached the edge of the bustle and strolled along the road between the sandy beach and the land. The smell of the sea spray was as good as any morning coffee. There were some trees along the shore, which gave some privacy to part of the road. This screen enabled one to focus on the view of the unbounded sea. The openness made her realise how unfettered she felt.

She was later than usual today, which meant she had lost the opportunity to see the mist emerging over the sea, and the early morning sky that sometimes resembled vanilla ice cream swirled with raspberry sauce.

Some surfers congregated on the sands, arms possessively stretched to full extent around surfboards as if they were a protective shield ready to defend them against a marauding, spear-wielding army. After their conference, they waded into the sea, which was flexing its muscles in great, bulging waves. The surfers rode the waves as naturally as Gaby had walked the village mountains. People were arriving sporadically, but she felt a slight unease at the man she saw walking from the opposite direction.

The first thing she noticed was his attire. He was dressed in some form of tweed, which was unfamiliar in these parts—the climate did not lend itself to such material. He also had a cloth cap, which was as glaring as a police siren. He was not very tall, but was stocky, with the wide-legged gait of a farmer. This may not have been so out of the ordinary in the sheep-shearing parts of the country. The few other people he passed, however, did not seem to display any curious attention. They did not even seem to notice he was there! Maybe there was some sort of theatre production around. Gaby comforted herself with this thought and sat on a wall that was low on the roadside, but there was a drop of about ten feet onto the beachside. She didn't want to go any further, as she would leave the sight of other people.

The peculiarly dressed man came and sat alongside her, which caused her unease to return. She looked anxiously around and noticed how few people were near. She looked towards the surfers with anticipation, and nervously wondered whether she would be in their sight.

'You're not from these parts, are yer?' His accent was Australian.

'How do you know?' she answered tensely.

There was a flicker of recognition, which Gaby dismissed instantly. *That's impossible*, she thought.

'I could just tell,' he replied dismissively.

She touched her brooch, which she often did in times of discomfort or distress. Maybe it was some form of assurance, a sense of security that her loved ones were near her.

'That brooch,' he said. 'Is it Celtic?'

'Yes.'

'You Welsh?'

She nodded silently.

'Oh, whereabouts?' He looked interested.

'Brynhalig.'

'Really!' His face registered recognition.

Again, she nodded.

'You ever heard of the Ty Coch murder?'

She went rigid, and all she could do was nod again, dumbfounded.

He seemed to puff up with pride.

'I did it.' He stood up with immediacy whilst jerking his thumb to his chest. He then swaggered off in his sideways, loping stride, leaving Gaby staring speechlessly after him until he disappeared around the corner.

Despite her stupefaction, she ran after him and stopped immediately on rounding the corner. She looked ahead and around in bewilderment. There was no sign of him. But that was impossible—where could he have got to in ten seconds? There was nowhere in the vicinity that would have provided cover. There was no one around, apart from a man and woman in about their fifties, dressed in typical, light, Australian dress, walking up the road in the only direction the peculiar man could have taken.

'You alright?' asked the man on getting closer. 'You look like you've seen a ghost.'

'Did you see anyone just now? Did anyone pass you—a man in thick tweeds?'

'No—no one's been here, and we've been walking this road for the past fifteen minutes. Strewth, in tweeds! Wouldn't have survived that long, lady.'

They continued on their way, and left Gaby staring into the distance. Gaby heard him saying to the woman, on thinking they were out of earshot, 'These Poms, can't take the sun.'

# Author Profile

I live in Cardiff with my husband, but I am originally from the South Wales Valleys. My writing started as an idea inspired by an actual event, which grew into a novel. I have brought my love of the Valleys landscape into my writing, but I also aim to challenge my readers, so I would not describe my work as mainstream.

I work as a Civil Servant. I enjoy films, books, travel and walks in the country. I have done voluntary work for an organisation providing food for the homeless in Cardiff.

## Publisher Information

Rowanvale Books provides publishing services to independent authors, writers and poets all over the globe. We deliver a personal, honest and efficient service that allows authors to see their work published, while remaining in control of the process and retaining their creativity. By making publishing services available to authors in a cost-effective and ethical way, we at Rowanvale Books hope to ensure that the local, national and international community benefits from a steady stream of good quality literature.

For more information about us, our authors or our publications, please get in touch.

www.rowanvalebooks.com
info@rowanvalebooks.com

Lightning Source UK Ltd.
Milton Keynes UK
UKHW041449071218
333642UK00001B/93/P